Tonight Only

I0635186

Alyse Zaftig

ISBN-13: 978-1-63481-039-5

CONTENTS

First Day

Catherine

I had butterflies in my stomach.

"Mom, I think that it might be better if I skip school this year. What if you homeschool me?"

"Honey, you're going to be fine, Kitty Cat. Don't worry about it. Everyone will love you."

I had serious doubts about that. I had never been popular anywhere, and I knew that this place would not necessarily be different. Really, all I would expect would be more of the same.

I'd be the strange new girl, too shy to talk to anybody. It was the same story in every new school. My stomach felt like snakes were slithering around.

I finished a glass of milk, and I put my backpack on. My mom had decided that we should be in an apartment that was within walking distance of school. She thought it was convenient, but it wasn't that great to be near the high school. If it was right there all the time, it was hard to forget about it.

I had gotten my class schedule in the mail, and I had gone to the bookstore to pick up my books the week before. I had everything in my backpack, and it felt like I had five bowling balls in there.

When I walked to school for my first class, I noticed a lot of people were turning around. I guessed that they hadn't seen someone like me before. I had always been awkward looking, but it was even worse now. My body was growing, and not all of it was growing at the same rate. I ducked my head, embarrassed to my toes by all of the attention. I hated being the new girl.

I sat down in my first class, English literature. Instantly, about five guys sat down around me. I felt like the center of a flower. It was weird. Even though I was not stick-thin, the guys around me had shoulders twice as wide as mine. They all looked like football players, and I was intimidated by the popular kids sitting by me. Were they going to turn this into *Carrie*?

One of them had more courage than the others. He leaned over and gave me a killer smile. He had dark chocolate eyes, and he was one of the most handsome guys that I had ever seen outside of a magazine or a movie.

"Hello!" He sounded nice and friendly, and I couldn't help but smile at him. "I'm Ryan. What's your name?"

I crossed my arms. "My name is Catherine. It's nice to meet you, Ryan."

"It's nice to meet you too, Catherine."

The teacher came in, and the classroom got quiet. I was nervous about the teacher deciding to introduce me to everyone, like a shiny new toy at show and tell, but the teacher had no interest in it. We drove straight into the syllabus for the year. I was so grateful to be going to public school. The last time, my mom had sent me to a private Christian school. Every person in it had been in the same class forever. I didn't fit in at all, and it was weird that everybody knew my name. At a public high school, I was able to be anonymous.

The rest of the day was exactly like that. The guys sat around me, and I was the object of several jealous glares from other girls. I would be lying if I said that I didn't enjoy the attention.

I'd never been a beauty queen, and my forehead was too large. My nose was too pointy. Somehow, none of the guys seemed to care about it. They acted like I was as beautiful as Naomi Campbell. They were attracted to me like magpies to a shiny object.

At the end of the school day, I finally found my locker. I was confused by the directions on the letter that I had received. I knew I should have walked around school before it started, but somehow, I had found people who wanted to help me get to my classes everywhere. Every single person who acted as a tour guide was male. I finally unloaded my heavy backpack, and I put the text books that I didn't need back into my locker. As soon as I closed my locker, I looked up.

There was a really tall guy. He was easily over six-foot-five, and he looked like the guy who would be a star basketball player. Unlike all the other guys, he didn't immediately introduce himself. In fact, I don't know if he even noticed me. He closed his locker, and I stayed by my open locker.

I stood there like a dope for a minute. I closed my locker, and I hurried home. My mom and I were low on groceries. At eighteen, I definitely needed to shoulder some of the responsibilities in the household. My mom worked all the time, and it was still barely enough. I always wanted to get a job, but my mom didn't want me to work. She said that going to school was my job. I tried to help by doing the dishes, taking out the trash, mowing the lawn when we had one, and doing the cooking. Last night, we had run out of the last box of spaghetti, and I needed to make sure that we didn't starve.

Groceries

Catherine

Three hours after I got home, my mom came home.

She looked completely exhausted, tired to the bone, but she put on a smile for me when she saw me chilling in the living room.

"Hello, honey. How was your first day of school?"

"It was good."

"Sweetheart, I'm going to take a nap before I fall over. Could you get dinner ready? I think I'm going to sleep for a few hours. Have you done your homework?"

"Yeah, my homework is done." I didn't tell her that nobody assigned homework on the first day of school. Nobody was that cruel and unusual, although my English literature teacher came the closest. He had told us that it would be good for us to get a head start on the first book, *Hamlet.*

"I'm going to drive to the grocery store and pick up some food. Do you want anything in particular?" I took the grocery list off of the refrigerator.

"No, honey, I'm sure that whatever you pick will be fine." She kissed my cheek. "I feel like you get more and more mature every day. It feels like you were my little baby girl only yesterday, and now you are shopping for the family. Thank you, sweetheart."

I kissed her cheek, then I took her car keys off of her keychain. I headed to the grocery store that was two miles away.

When I turned on the car, it roared to life. It was easily ten years old, although we didn't know the exact age. It was enough to get us around, and my mom hadn't had the money to have the oil changed in a while. The check engine light was on, but we just ignored it. We didn't have the luxury of bringing it to the mechanic every time the check engine light went on. It was buggy anyway.

I went to the grocery store and picked up everything on the list. Why was it that everything that I needed was always in the back corner?

When I hit the frozen aisle, I picked up a half-gallon of chocolate gelato. It was an indulgence, but it was a small luxury that we could afford. I knew that my mom could probably use some chocolate gelato after her day, and I could certainly use it after mine. It was surreal to be here, because everybody paid attention to me. I was more of the wallflower who tried to fade into the background, and it looked like I wouldn't be able to when I was here.

I paid for everything with my debit card. My mom had got me one when I was thirteen, because in a single-parent household, there were times when she wouldn't be able to find cash lying around the house.

The bagger asked me, "Do you need help with that?" There was a note of hope in his voice, as if he really wanted to help me bring my groceries to my car.

"Nope, I'm good."

I pushed my cart out of the store to go to my car. The car was so old that I had to unlock the trunk in order to open it. I was envious of everybody who just had it automatically open for them. Life could be so easy in a lot of ways, if only we had the money for it.

I was most of the way home when I heard an ominous sound, a little rattling under the hood. The car stopped. I turned the wheel so that it would go towards the ditch on the side of the road.

I felt my eyes fill with tears, and one of them dropped. Tears wouldn't solve anything, I told myself. You need to get this show on the road. I was about a mile away from home, and I was certainly close enough to get help. My mom and I would figure out a way to make this work. By the time I got home, though, the gelato would probably melt.

I got out of the car, but a large, dark blue SUV was coming and parking behind me. I hoped it wasn't an ax murderer. Maybe it was somebody with a cell phone. I didn't have one, because we couldn't afford it. My mom didn't have one.

I was surprised when I saw who came out. I looked up. Way up.

Stranded

Kyle

I got out of my SUV, and I went to help the stranded motorist. When she got out of the car, I felt like someone sucker punched me. It was that new girl, the one who had a locker near mine.

I noticed her, like everybody noticed her. She was hot, and she was new.

I would be more interested, except it looked like I would be competing against half of the senior class. I wasn't interested in that kind of competition.

I walked over.

"Hey, can I help?"

I saw her shoulders slump, and her cheeks got red.

"My car broke down."

"That's okay. I can get you home. Don't you have a cell phone?"

Her shoulders slumped even further.

"No."

It was a very short answer, but it told me a lot. She was a little too defensive, crossing her arms and giving me a glare, and I backed off.

"Well, I can drive you wherever you need to go."

She rubbed the back of her neck. "I have a favor to ask."

"What?"

"I'm coming home from the grocery store, so I have gelato in the back. I just don't want it to melt. Would it be okay if I transferred my groceries into your car?"

"Yeah, no problem."

She unlocked her trunk, and she pushed it open. I took her grocery bags out, and the two of us reloaded my car with her groceries.

"Wow, do you shop for your entire family? My mom tends to be the one who does it. I don't think she would trust me with it."

She looked at her feet, and I got the impression that I should just stop asking questions.

"Yes, I do shop for my entire family, but it's only two people," she said quietly.

She went to lock her car, and I closed my trunk. This was obviously a touchy subject, so I wanted to leave it alone. She got in the passenger side, and I couldn't help but notice how beautiful her curves were. She was everything I liked in a girl, but I knew that hundreds of other boys felt the same way. They didn't have her in their passenger seat, though. I was smug, although I wasn't really part of this competition.

"Where do you live?"

"I live in Parker Lane, which is really close. You just go another mile down the road, and then you turn on Walnut. It's on your right, so you can't miss it."

"Sounds great."

When we got to her apartment, I told her, "I will help you unload."

"Thanks."

She smiled at me as if she hadn't expected me to help. I was a little bit angry. What did she think that I would do? Just dump her and the groceries and then leave?

She went to her apartment, and she unlocked the door.

An older version of her came to the door.

"Do you need help unloading the groceries, sweetie?"

Her mom did a double take when she saw me.

"Oh, honey, I didn't know that you were with a friend. Who is this?"

"Hello, I am Kyle Richards." I extended my hand, and her mother shook it. She had a nice, firm grip.

"I'm only here because I rescued the damsel in distress."

"Oh no, what happened?"

"The car broke down on the side of the road, Mom."

Her mother's face fell. I realized that two people who couldn't afford cell phones, which I considered a basic necessity of life, probably couldn't afford to pay for a car repair. I knew approximately how much that would cost, since my dad owned two garages in town.

"You know what? I've been working on cars since I was a little kid. My dad is a mechanic, and I'm sure that I can get some tools. I can fix it for you for free, if you want."

"We would love your help." Her mom gave me a hug. I accepted it, even though we were basically strangers. She smelled nice, like cinnamon.

Catherine and I brought all the groceries into the apartment, and then her mom started cooking. There was only one more bag left, and Catherine walked with me to my car to pick it up. She grabbed it first.

It was a heavy bag, one with a milk jug in it, and I wanted to bring it into the house for her.

"Can I take that for you?" I would take any excuse to spend more time with this beautiful girl.

"No, I'm fine." She balanced the bag on a hip. "See?"

A gust of wind blew hair across her face, and I tucked it behind her ear. She had gorgeous dark eyes, and I leaned in for a quick kiss. I surprised myself. I normally didn't kiss on the first date, and this wasn't even a first date. I was just helping her with her groceries.

I leaned her back, and I liked the way that her eyes were fully closed. I broke the kiss. It was short and sweet, but it was definitely the nicest kiss I'd ever had.

"I'll see you tomorrow. My mom wanted me to help with dinner today." I got into my car, and I watched in my rearview mirror as she walked back into her apartment slowly, like a sleepwalker.

Illusions Shattered

Catherine

I stayed up all night thinking about Kyle's kiss. It was the first time that anybody had kissed me, and I liked it. I walked to school with a bounce in my step.

I went to my locker first thing in the morning in order to see him. What would it be like? I blushed a little thinking about the heat that had made my toes curl yesterday.

I waited at my locker. I smiled when I saw him coming, but then I saw a cheerleader named Lana jump on to him. He caught her, and she kissed him hard, shoving her tongue into his open mouth.

I went to the bathroom and tried not to cry. I didn't know who this girl was, but obviously she had more claim on him then some girl that he took pity on and drove home. He probably got way too many girls to count.

I had to stay away from players like this. If he could get to me within twenty-four hours, who knew just how many girls that he had in his harem?

I went through the day in a daze. I had started the day with so many hopes, but they were all crushed before first period. So, I was pretty surprised when Kyle showed up at my house that afternoon.

He knocked on my door, and we could see each other through the window that was next to the door. But I wouldn't open it. He waited for a minute, and then he walked to the car. Even though I refused to talk to him, he was going to fix it. He pulled apart some stuff, and he had the hood open. I watched him, and I wished that I still had the right to speak to him. But I knew that whoever that girl was it would probably tear my head off if I tried to make a move on him.

It would be healthier for my social life if I stayed away from cheerleaders' boyfriends. At my old schools, the cheerleaders ruled the roost; it was a very bad idea to cross them.

Fixing the Car

Kyle

It was weird. She wouldn't open the door. When we kissed last night, she seemed like she was into it. I hadn't seen her at school today, but I looked for her. She stood out of the crowd, because all the guys looked her way. But it was as if she were a ghost. I wanted to get to know Catherine better, but my ex-girlfriend Lana called me.

"Hey. You want to hang out?"

"I'm working on a car."

"Ok, I will come by your dad's shop. I can keep you company while you're working."

"No, I'm not at my dad's garage. I'm somewhere else."

I could hear a long pause. Then, Lana carefully asked, "Where are you?"

I thought about it for a half second. I wasn't going to give her a real answer. She had been crazy jealous while we were together, and I didn't want to think about what she would do to the new girl if she knew that I was at her house. She had basically jumped on me this morning, kissing me before I could react, but I set her straight. I told her that I wasn't interested, but she was very interested in getting back together. I knew that she would keep trying.

* * *

Life went on like this for a few weeks. Lana kept calling me every single afternoon while I fixed the car. She was very curious. I was glad that I wasn't on the football team anymore, because I would not have time to do this if I had to go to practice. Catherine wouldn't speak to me, and I still never ran into her in school. It seemed like we didn't have any classes together, and even though our lockers were close to each other, she somehow figured out a way to never be at her locker when I was at mine. Maybe she was just carrying all of her text books all the time.

When the car was done, I knocked on the door. I was sweaty, and I had grease all over me.

My dad approved of a man getting his hands dirty. When the subject came up at the dinner table — my mom was as sharp as a tack, and she could see how dirty my hands were, even if she was sick — I told him I was fixing a car for a girl, and he just winked at me knowingly.

Her mom answered the door this time.

"I am done fixing the car. Would you like to see it?"

I knew that her mom must be getting to work another way, although I had no idea how.

"I've been taking the bus everyday, but it only leaves once per hour. I've had to get up way earlier than I would if I could use the car. I'm really looking forward to being able to drive to work again."

I felt like a heel for not working on it faster. I had worked on it as much as I could, but this lady had to wake up early in order to get to work.

I went and started the engine. It roared to life, and it didn't have any of the weird squeaks that it would have if I had taken most of it apart.

Her mom put her hands over her mouth. She looked happy, as if she had just won the lottery.

She hugged me carefully, trying not to get any of the grease from me on to her. I hugged her with my wrist, because my hands were dirty.

"Let's go out for ice cream," she said. "It'll be my treat."

"My hands are too dirty to go to an ice cream place right now."

"Oh, that's fine. You can wash up inside. We should get Catherine anyway."

I didn't know if Catherine would go at all...she was definitely a master at disappearing. We went inside of their home. It was small, but it was bright and cheerful.

"Catherine," her mother said. "I'm so happy! Kyle fixed the car, and I'll be able to drive to work again. Isn't that wonderful?"

"Yeah, that's wonderful. Thanks, Kyle." She wouldn't meet my eyes.

I cleared my throat. "Is there a sink where I could wash up?"

"Yes." She pointed to the sink. "You might want to use dishwashing soap, because that is some pretty thick grease."

I went to the sink, and I used their apple-scented dishwashing soap. I spent some time getting the dirt from under my fingernails. I was sure that Catherine and her mom didn't care, but I did.

"Catherine, we are going out for ice cream."

"I'm not hungry."

"Catherine Jackson," her mother hissed. "You are going out for ice cream now. You barely get out of the house, and this is a good opportunity."

I kept washing my hands, pretending like I couldn't hear this private conversation. I knew that Catherine didn't want to go out with me, but it looked like her mother would make her. I would take it. I knew it wasn't the smoothest thing, but I definitely needed all the help I could get with her. For some reason, it seemed like she wasn't eager to spend any time with me. After our first kiss, I thought that we would be seeing a lot more of each other. I wanted to date her. But I had been here for weeks, and she never came out of her apartment.

"I'll get my purse, and I can meet you two outside." Her mother went into her bedroom, and Catherine and I were left facing each other, all alone in the room.

"Let's go." I gestured with my head towards the door.

Ice Cream

Kyle

"Thanks for fixing the car," she said stiffly.

"No problem," I said, even though I had sacrificed many afternoons to work for free. It had been worth it to spend even a little time with Catherine. I didn't get why I never saw her at school.

We all got in the car, and I drove to the nearest place. It was called Sweet Berries, and it had the best ice cream in the area. It was the most expensive place, too, but that was because they served thick, sweet custard, not ice cream.

Mrs. Jackson looked at the prices, a little bit shell shocked.

"Wow, this place is more expensive than any ice cream place I've ever been to."

"Not a problem," I said smoothly. "I can pay for it."

"You aren't paying for it." Catherine had a defiant gleam in her eye. "We don't need your charity."

"Catherine! Stop being so rude. It's a gentleman's prerogative to help us out. If he wants to take us out for ice cream, it's certainly acceptable. It's like your first date." She smiled at me hopefully. My dad wasn't the only one who could understand what it meant for me to spend every afternoon working on the car.

"I don't even know what's good here. I haven't ever been here before, and I'm unlikely to ever come here again," Catherine said.

"That's cool. You should really try their specialty, their monster custard, if you won't be here again."

When we got to the head of the line, I ordered three monster custards. I prayed that they wouldn't look at the menu, because it was the most expensive thing on it. It was the specialty of the store. The entire Sweet Berries empire had been built on the strength of selling people custard that was way too expensive.

We waited on the other side of the counter for them to give us our monster custard.

They gave it to us pretty quickly, and we all sat down at the table closest to the door. Cat looked jittery, like she would run out the door at the earliest opportunity.

We quietly finished our ice cream, and we were about to go when the door swung open.

Lana came in.

"Oh," she said, looking at me with Catherine and her mom. "I didn't know that you were into threesomes, Kyle."

I gritted my teeth. "Lana, I would like you to meet Catherine and her mother."

"Her mom?" Lana snorted. "That's definitely her older sister. Don't try to fool me now, Kyle. I know you're a freak, remember?" She winked.

I could feel my face turning red, and Catherine put her right hand over her eyes. Her mother was less embarrassed, but she didn't have to go to school the next day.

"Well, don't let me spoil your fun." Lana smirked at me. I knew that I would have to do damage control the next day, but I didn't care. It was worth it. I wanted to do something nice for Catherine and her mother, and taking them out for frozen custard was a good choice, no matter if Lana wanted to spoil it.

"See you," I told her.

I pushed the door open, and the three of us went into the newly fixed car.

"Who was that?"

"That's Lana, a cheerleader." I answered as briefly as I could. I didn't tell the Jacksons that Lana was my former girlfriend. Our relationship ended when I caught her cheating on me with one of the other guys on the football team. She had been so blasé about being caught that I knew that she didn't really care about our relationship.

I dropped Catherine and her mother off at home. Catherine went out the door as soon as the car stopped, but her mom stopped and told me, "Thank you for spending so much time on the car. I know that you've been here every day, and I just wish that I could have baked you brownies or something everyday. I've been working, and the bus takes me home an hour after I get off of work, and I've missed you every time."

"Well, I hope that you'll have more time at home. Take care. You and your daughter are special people."

She hugged me, and I hugged her back.

"I'll see you around." I watched her go back into her apartment.

I got into my SUV, and I drove off.

Mama Knows Best

Catherine

"Well," my mama said. "That boy is certainly sweet on you."

I felt my face flush. "No, Mom, it's not like that. He's one of the most popular guys at school. He barely notices that I'm alive. I have no idea why he wanted to fix our car. Maybe he wanted a challenge or something. He's way out of my league."

"Now, I may be an old lady, but I think that you're a beautiful girl. I don't see any problems with you dating him. If you want to date him, I give you my blessing."

"Mom, it's not that simple. He's in a different stratosphere."

"Well," my mom said pensively. "You know, I remember what it was like to be in high school. I'm just going to tell you to go for what you want. You don't have to let his popularity stop you."

"Like that worked out so well for you. You married your high school sweetheart. Look where that got you. Divorced. Alone." I normally wasn't so cruel, but I wanted her to butt out of my social life.

"Hey," she told me softly. "Don't be nasty. I was just trying to be helpful. I loved your father very much. It's not really my fault that he turned out to be a criminal."

"Didn't it send off any warning signs when he already had a juvenile record? Who knew that he would get arrested when he was eighteen, leaving us alone? You had to deal with your pregnancy by yourself. Wouldn't it be nice if I could actually have the support of someone else? I think that Kyle is a player, and I have no intention of being a teen mom."

"Well, baby girl, if you got pregnant, you would always have me. I wouldn't throw you out of the house like my parents did."

I felt all the anger drain out of me. I knew that my mother loved me unconditionally, even when I was being mean. "Thank you, Mama. I love you." I blew her a kiss. I knew that she was just trying to help.

"You're welcome, baby. Now, I'm not hungry for dinner. We shouldn't have sugar for dinner every night, but I don't think that we need to cook tonight."

"Totally," I agreed.

I went up to my room and thought about Kyle. If I had seen him with Lana, I wouldn't know about his reputation. The way that nobody had reacted in the hallway meant that they were used to Lana and Kyle acting like that. I wasn't experienced at all, and I wasn't ready for mind games. It was better if I stayed away from Kyle.

Prom

Kyle

MAY

"Fine," I told Lana. "I'll go to the prom with you."

She clapped her hands and jumped up and down.

"Oh, I'm so happy. I have to go shopping right away."

I knew that she already had a dress. Lana had been on me to take her to the dance for two months, but I still held out hope that I would be able to go with Catherine.

Yesterday, Ryan told me that he was taking Catherine to the prom. He'd gotten a lot of high fives for being the first to convince Catherine to date him. It was clear that she was on the market. She just wasn't up for dating me. She was a ghost. I didn't think that she even went to her locker.

I was quickly proven wrong when I heard a locker slam behind me.

I turned around to see Catherine, her eyes wide. It was the first time that I'd seen her at her locker since the first week of school.

"Catherine, wait!"

But she fled, and I couldn't follow her in the crowded hallway. It was the worst timing ever, and I wondered if Lana had planned it like that. But how could she? How would she know when Catherine went to her locker?

I slammed my locker shut. I had to go to class before the bell, or I would've tried to find her.

* * *

I was uncomfortable in my rented tux. Lana had chosen the color, and I wasn't in black like everybody else. She was wearing pure white, so she wanted me to wear a blue suit so that we would have stunning, somewhat unique pictures. She said that she wanted me to be visible in a sea of black and white. I shrugged. I didn't care what I wore.

My mom took pictures of us in the foyer. I knew that she didn't approve of Lana, because she didn't think that she was good enough for me. However, I didn't know who my mom would think was good enough for me, so it was useless to try to please her.

I had to give this much to her, though. My mom had breast cancer, and we didn't know how long she would live. It was in remission now, but it was a battle that taught me that there was no amount of money that could buy health. We had enough money to buy every treatment for her, but it wasn't enough.

So my mom was too thin, and I stood there as she took a million pictures of me and my date.

Finally, a limo came to the curb outside. I got in there. Ryan and Catherine were already inside, in addition to Adriana and Matthew.

"You all look so nice!" Catherine said.

"You all? Are you southern?" Lana sneered.

"Hey," I said, the warning clear in my voice. "Play nice. Sheathe your claws."

Lana shut up, but she put her hand on my arm, like I belonged to her. I shrugged her off. She frowned, but she leaned back in her seat.

Ryan had his hand on Catherine's knee. She didn't make a move to pull it off, but she didn't look all that comfortable, either.

When we got to prom, we had to take more pictures. We took some as a group of six. And then, we took some with just two people. Lana honestly could have stayed there all night, posing away like a model. We were the last ones to go.

By the time that we left, I couldn't see the other people in our group. They were probably dancing.

All the girls were dancing in a manner completely inappropriate for the evening gowns that they were wearing. The guys were standing around awkwardly, swaying to the music.

I looked around. I couldn't find Catherine in the mass of moving bodies. Where was she?

I finally saw her. She was running out one of the doors. When a woman ran in heels, something was probably wrong.

"I'll be right back," I promised Lana. She didn't appear to care. She was dancing with a bunch of other girls, with all of their dates in a circle around them, awkwardly fist-pumping.

I went out the same door that Catherine had.

Breaking Up

Catherine

"Come on," Ryan said. "It will be awesome."

"I don't think that I'm old enough to live with someone else," I told him.

"Plenty of people move in with each other in college. You're going to have a roommate anyway. Why not live together?"

"Because I don't think that I want to focus on you when I'm in college. I want to go to MIT, and you are going to Stanford. There's no way that it's going to work."

"You were accepted to Stanford, and you have a full ride. Why? Why don't you want to come with me?"

"I just prefer the physics program at MIT over the one at Stanford. You know that I visited both of them, and I know that the people at MIT would be a better fit for me."

"What about me?"

"You are incredibly interested in robotics. It's pretty clear that you should be a Stanford student."

"But I don't want to break up with you."

"We don't have to break up. We can have a long distance relationship," I said soothingly.

"No! I don't want to lose you. Come on, just come to Stanford with me. It'll be so much fun."

"No," I said. "I'm not going to go to Stanford."

"What? Am I not good enough for you?" Ryan was holding onto my arm, and he was squeezing me enough to make me a little uncomfortable. I pulled my arm out of his grip.

"No, you are being weird. I'm going to go to the right college for me, and you should go to the right college for you."

"Come on. I'm sure you can figure something out."

"No, I'm not going to come with you. If you're going to be like this, I don't want to even date you for the rest of senior year."

"What do you mean by that?"

"We're done."

I jumped back a foot as Ryan went to the nearby refreshment table and threw the punch bowl to the ground. Red punch went flying everywhere, and the glass bowl shattered into a thousand pieces.

He ran for the front door, so I went for a side door. A sign said "emergency exit" and I hoped that it wouldn't sound an alarm when I went through it.

I pushed my way into a small, dark alley. It was the kind of place that my mother had told me to be careful in. I didn't think that there would be too many people here. Anyways, there was security for the dance. The hotel security was probably good enough to keep major creepers away.

The door swung open behind me. My shoulders tensed up, because I didn't want to talk to Ryan anymore. I spun around.

It wasn't Ryan. It was Kyle.

Dark Alley

Kyle

"Hey," I said as I shoved my hands into my pockets. "I saw you run out of the room. Are you okay?"

Catherine started crying. I blinked, trying to think fast. I didn't like it when women cried. There was mascara running down her face.

"Hey...what's wrong?"

"I just broke up with Ryan."

"What do you mean? Did he just break up with you? At prom?"

"No. I just broke up with him."

"What happened?"

"He wants us to go to the same college, but I don't want to go to the West Coast. I would rather stay closer to home, and the physics program at MIT is a better fit for me. He doesn't see it like that. He keeps saying that I don't think that he's good enough for me."

"He is being absolutely ridiculous," I said. "Let me talk to him. I'm sure I can talk some sense into that boy."

"No, don't." Catherine stopped crying, and she wiped away her tears. "This is for the best."

"Can I take you home? I can call a taxi, and you don't have to stay here."

"That would be nice," Catherine said. "I must look like a mess."

I looked at her. She looked like a raccoon, but I wasn't going to say so. "I think you look beautiful," I said truthfully. Even with her makeup running down her face, she was still beautiful to me.

"That is very kind of you to say. I appreciate the sentiment, although I can't imagine that I look anything like a beautiful girl right now. I'm an ugly crier."

I took my phone out of my pocket, and I saw that there was an Uber just around the corner.

I hailed the Uber, and I pulled her towards the entrance of the alley. "Come on, there's a taxi coming in a minute."

We got to the street, and we didn't even wait a minute before the car came. I helped her into the car, and I went in after her.

"Where we heading?"

Catherine gave the driver her address, and we quietly left the dance. If the driver noticed her makeup running all over the place, he didn't say anything.

I texted Lana. *Hey, something came up. We are casual, anyway. Go home with whomever you want to.*

It wasn't like I needed any permission. We had a very casual relationship, and we had for the last several years. For some reason, she kept coming back for more. I never seriously dated her again, not after I found out that she was with my friend Kade, but she was a beautiful girl and she wanted to be with me...so I didn't resist too hard.

We went home, and I tipped the Uber guy. The company said that the gratuity was included, but that mostly meant that they took some part of it off of the top. The driver thanked me, and Catherine and I got out of the car.

"Come inside," Catherine said. "It's the least I can do. I can make us hot chocolate or something. I'm sorry that you're missing the after party because of my drama."

Hot Chocolate

Kyle

"There's no place that I'd rather be," I told her, the ring of truth clear in my voice. "If you point me to your hot chocolate mix, I can make it. You might want to run into a bathroom."

She pointed to the cabinet next to the far wall in the kitchen. "You'll find mugs and chocolate mix in there."

She headed into her bedroom, and I was opening the cabinet when I heard a scream.

I ran over to her bedroom door, worried that there was an intruder or something; she came out and glared at me, her eyes accusatory. "What the hell!? You told me I looked beautiful! I look like a troll monster on a bad hair day!"

"I'm going to plead the Fifth," I told her. "But at least I told you to go to the bathroom?"

"You're not getting off so easy, buster."

"You're beautiful, even when you look like a troll monster." I leaned down and kissed her nose. "Now kick off your high heels and wash all that makeup off. You'll have hot chocolate when you're done."

She went into her room and closed the door. I could hear water running, and I went to the kitchen to make hot chocolate.

I got the mugs out, and I put the mugs into the microwave at the same time, putting the hot chocolate in for an extra thirty seconds to handle the extra mass. It was strange to think of the times when I applied my thermodynamics lessons from AP Physics.

As it dinged, I heard her door open. I turned around with the warm mugs in my hands, and I almost dropped them.

She was dressed in a simple, lavender purple dress. Her hair was down and curling around her face. The dress had a V-neck; it wasn't meant to be revealing, but when a girl was as stacked as Catherine was, it definitely enhanced her assets. Her face was fresh and clean, but she was even more beautiful.

"I like you more like this," I confessed.

"What? This is a twenty-dollar nightgown from Target. I pretend it's a dress, but it's definitely not. Look at me. Look at you."

"This is a rented tux." I shrugged, careful not to spill the drinks.

"Yeah, but you guys have all kinds of money. Your dad is more than just a mechanic, isn't he?"

"He has two garages in town, if that's what you mean."

She gave me a stare.

"And several in different states around us." I squirmed. My dad actually owned a franchise, and he made a ton of money off of it. "It's not a big deal, though."

"I bet you don't live in an apartment."

"Well, no, I don't," I confessed. "But still, money isn't a huge thing."

"Only rich people can say that. I bet you don't have to check your bank balance before you go to the grocery store."

I didn't know what to say to that. I didn't, to be honest. My mom was the one who took care of groceries, but if I ever wanted anything, all I had to do was drive to the store and get it. I offered her a steaming mug of hot chocolate.

"I found marshmallows in that cabinet. Do you want a spoon to stir the marshmallows in?"

"Nah, I'm good." She took a sip and nearly spat it out. "What did you do? Put the chocolate in for five minutes?"

I took a sip of my chocolate. "It's lukewarm, not hot."

"Trade me," she demanded. She handed me her mug, and she took mine. We each took a sip.

"Oh my goodness," I yelped. "This is basically thermonuclear!"

She swallowed. "This is room temperature."

I looked at the microwave. "Oh..."

"What?"

"I didn't remember that you didn't have that spinning plate on the bottom of your microwave. Microwaves heat things unevenly. I'm sorry that I gave you such hot chocolate."

"That's okay." She put the mug down. "We're not really here for hot chocolate anyway."

"Oh?" I said, raising one of my eyebrows. "What are we here for?"

"To talk, of course." She wiped her palms on her dress. "Let's tell each other stuff."

"You've been avoiding me all year, and you want to talk to me now? What's changed?"

"Well, for one thing, I'm not dating Ryan right now."

"Yeah, that's a good thing."

"And for another, you've finally caught me. I've tried to stay away from you, but that's definitely been unsuccessful."

"Well, okay. I mean, most of this year has been eaten up by my mother's illness."

"Your mother is sick? With what?"

"Breast cancer."

She gasped. "I'm so sorry."

I shrugged. "I'm used to it now. And she is in remission at the moment. They'll periodically check her to make sure that it doesn't come back, but we're just taking each day as it comes."

"Still, that has to be hard for you and your dad."

"If it's hard on my dad, I can't tell. He's gone most of the time, anyway. It's me and my mom." I shrugged again. "Tell me what you're doing after high school."

"I'm going to MIT, and I'm going to major in physics. I specifically have an interest in astrophysics, and I think that I'm going to pursue that all the way to my PhD."

"That sounds great. I think that you are way more highly motivated than I am," I told her. "All I want to do is join the military."

"The military?" she asked. "I didn't peg you for a military man."

I shrugged for a third time. "My mom's dad was an admiral, and we know some senators. They wrote letters of recommendation for me to go to West Point."

"West Point? That's prestigious."

I looked down. "It's okay, I guess. My mom wanted to throw me this huge party, but I convinced her not to. I didn't want anybody to make a big deal about it. It's not a huge thing."

"Well, if you're going to West Point, you're going to be on the East Coast."

"Yes, but I don't think that we'd see each other that often. It's in upstate New York, and you're going to be outside of Boston."

"We could make it work."

I shook my head. "The first year at West Point...the summer training...I don't think that I could have a girlfriend while I went through the Beast Barracks."

She was quiet for a moment, and then she said, "That's okay. We could keep it light and casual. Just for tonight. Tonight only."

I licked my lips. She leaned towards me. "When is your mom getting home?"

"She's not. She's out of town on a business trip. There's some conference in Oregon that she wanted to go to, so I'm home alone. I turned nineteen last month, so it's not a big deal."

"I'm nineteen, too, and my parents would never leave me alone for that long. That's not safe," I teased. "I better keep you company, then."

I pulled her curvy body into my arms, and I kissed her like I had wanted to for an entire school year. I kissed her hard, and her mouth opened beneath mine.

"Do you want this?"

"Yes," she whispered.

Tonight Only

Kyle

I picked her up, her legs wrapped around me, and we went to her bedroom. I threw her on the bed, and I peeled her nightgown off.

She was fully shaven down there, and I went to worship between her legs.

She pulled her thick thighs together and tried to get away, but I put a hand on her thighs to keep her right there.

"What's the matter? Shy? Self-conscious?" I looked at her body. "You have nothing to be self-conscious about."

"I just..." She closed her eyes. "I've never done this before."

"Gotten head? What, have guys been inconsiderate with you?"

Her eyes were still shut. "No, I've never done this before. At all."

"You're a virgin?" I heard my voice crack on that last word. I was the furthest thing from a virgin imaginable.

"Yes."

I backed up. "Maybe this isn't a good idea. I can call a cab, and we can..."

She got off the bed, and she put her hand on my arm. "No, please. I want this."

"If you're sure."

In response, she pulled me back on the bed. She spread her thighs, and I'd never seen anything more erotic than her untouched body as she offered herself to me.

I pushed her thighs further apart, and I started with slow, smooth licks. I rubbed her clit with one of my thumbs, and her body writhed beneath mine. I was hard enough to pound nails, but tonight was all about her. I had been given an extraordinary gift, and I wasn't about to waste it.

She bucked beneath me as she went through her first orgasm, but I didn't stop. I kept stimulating her, and I watched as she shook through a second and then a third orgasm.

She pushed my head away. "Stop," she said weakly. "I can't take anymore. I'm going to die. It's too much."

"Darling, I'm just getting started. But don't worry. I'll do all the work. Okay?"

"Okay," she whispered.

I stood up, and I took off my stupid blue tux. I hated it, and it was uncomfortable to be restrained by my pants. Her eyes widened as I moved towards her, naked and ready to take her. Her eyes were glued to my enlarged cock, and I stroked it.

"Like what you see?"

"That's not going to fit inside of my body, no matter how many orgasms I've been through." She shut her thighs. "It hurts to even put tampons in there."

"Don't worry," I soothed. "I'll be gentle with you."

I got on all fours above her, and I coaxed her mouth open. We kissed, and I felt myself get impossibly harder and longer. I was dripping precome now, and I could feel a little bit getting on her bare skin.

I went down and kissed and bit her neck, and she shivered.

"You like that?"

She pulled my head close. I guessed she did.

I went down again, and I started biting the slopes of her breasts. She cried out beneath me, and somebody thumped on the ceiling.

"Keep it quiet down there."

I held back a laugh. There would be a lot more thumping before the night was through.

I sat on the bed, and I pulled her into my lap, with her legs on either side of me.

"Are you ready?" I murmured, biting her ear as I whispered in it.

"Yes," she told me.

I put a hand on my cock, and I guided it to her wet entrance. After so many orgasms and a lot of foreplay, I knew that she definitely would be ready.

I pushed the head in, and she gasped. Her eyes were wide with wonder.

"You like that?"

"Yes," she said, and she ground her hips on me.

"Okay, Catherine, you're going to have to slow down, or this is all going to be over way before it really gets started."

"I'm ready now." With that, she forced my cock inside of her, as deep as it could possibly go.

We both cried out then, and there was more thumping from above. It just made me grin, and Catherine bit my shoulder.

"We have to be quiet," Catherine said. "Our landlady lives up there."

I put a finger on my lips. "I'll be quiet," I whispered to her.

I kissed her mouth, and I fucked her with my tongue and cock at the same time. I had my hands on her hips, pulling her into me. She was the most beautiful woman in the world, and she had given me the gift of her virginity. I was determined to make this night the best of her life. You never forget your first, and I needed to make this a night that she would always remember fondly.

"Does it hurt?" I heard that girls sometimes hurt when they had their first times.

"No," she said, and she fluttered around me. "I feel like I'm melting inside like milk chocolate left in the sun."

"Good." I bit her neck, and I buried my face at the juncture of her neck and shoulder. I picked up the pace, and she moaned as I pulled her up and down my cock.

"I'm going to blow," I warned.

"Me, too," she answered. That was enough to push me over the edge, and we spiraled into infinity together.

When I could move again, I opened my eyes. My arms were locked around her, and I tried to loosen them. I couldn't.

"I want to let you go, but I can't."

"It's okay." She leaned into me a little more. "I like being like this." She kissed me softly, and I returned her gentle kiss. We were like that for several minutes before my muscles loosened enough to let her go.

I pulled her off of my softening cock, but I wasn't ready to really let go of her yet.

"You cleaned up, but I didn't. You're dirty again anyway. I think I need to wash you. All over."

I scooted to the edge of the bed, and I picked her up.

"You've got to stop picking me up like this. I am too big."

"Too big? You're just right. I could carry you for a daylong hike and not feel it. I'm pretty sure my hiking backpack weighs more than you."

She looked like she didn't believe me, so I just kissed that expression right off of her face.

We went into her bathroom, and I turned on the water with one hand, while I kept her balanced on my hip. I stepped into the shower, and both of us were instantly drenched. The sweat and juices were washed away. I pinned her against the wall, and her back was flat against the tile.

I kissed her again and again, and I could feel myself coming back to life. It seemed like the first round wasn't enough; my body wanted more from her. I wanted more than one night, but I would take what I could get.

I guided my cock into her, and she was a little looser than the first time, but she was still tight. I wanted to spend the rest of my life like this, and it seemed like a cruel joke that I'd finally get what I wanted when both of us were out of time. I had to leave for summer training way too soon.

I thrust into her, and she moaned in front of me. I crashed into her like an ocean wave hitting the shore, never letting up.

This time, it wasn't as fast as the first one. I was sweeter with her, more tender. I swiveled my hips between strokes, and she liked it.

I bit her shoulder as I exploded inside of her, and she shivered as she orgasmed in my arms, milking my cock of everything that it still held inside. I spurted in her again.

My legs felt like golden jelly after I came, and I put her on her feet. "I don't think I have the strength to stand up right now." I turned off the water and sat on the ledge in her shower. "I don't know if I'll be able to walk for another week, to be honest."

She giggled. "Let's towel off."

She got out of the shower, and she snagged a towel off of the rack. I liked the way that she dried me, especially since she followed the towel with kisses.

I got out of the shower, and I dried the rest of myself off. We were naked and totally unashamed as we slept in her bed. My parents wouldn't expect me home until tomorrow morning — the after parties at my school were legendary for going past dawn — and I went and set an alarm on my phone for four hours from now.

"I want to hold you," I told her.

She lay on her side in her bed, and I spooned her. It wasn't a big bed, but we just barely fit. I pulled her hair to the side, and I nuzzled her warm neck. My eyes drooped, and they closed.

Warm and happy with her in the circle of my arms, I fell asleep.

Morning After

Kyle

When I woke up, she wasn't in bed. The pillow next to mine was still warm when I checked, though, so I knew that she hadn't been gone for long. I found my pants and put them on. I went out to her living room.

"Good morning," she said.

I flashed a grin at her. "Good morning." I bent down to kiss her, but she turned so that I kissed her cheek instead.

"One night only, remember?"

"Right."

I turned and went back into her bedroom. I got properly dressed in the tux again. I looked at myself in her bathroom mirror. I looked the same — maybe a little more disheveled — but I felt different. Something that night had changed me. I went to my phone, and I called an Uber. It would be there in five minutes.

I went back out to the main room, and I realized that she was fully dressed. "Are you ready for the day, then?"

"Yeah, I am." I nodded. I guessed that our night was really over.

"Well, I really enjoyed your company. I wish that we had gotten together earlier, but..."

She walked forward and hugged me. "Me, too. I was pigheaded. But I'm glad that you spent last night with me. I'll never forget it."

I heard a honk from outside. Like a ninja, I stole a kiss, and then I was out the door. As I got into the car, I turned around. She was standing at the window with a hand rubbing the center of her chest. I raised a hand to say goodbye. I wished that I didn't have to go to West Point. If I didn't join the military, all of this would be different. She could be my girl. We'd spend the summer exploring each other.

But it was useless to wish that I were another person with another life. The Uber took me home, and I thanked him with some cash before I got out. My parents were still asleep, and I went to my room to get dressed again. There was a fee for returning the tux too late, and I might as well get it done. I was too keyed up to go to sleep. I dressed in a polo and khakis, and then I drove down to the mall.

I ducked inside of Men's Wearhouse, which had just opened, and I gave them back the tux.

Without the tux, it was like last night had never happened. I probably had a few bite marks, but they would fade with time. It was like a magical moment that didn't exist in time. She wasn't my girlfriend; I wasn't her boyfriend. And I knew that in reality, Lana would be on me yet again. But it was nice to pretend, if only for a matter of hours, that I could be together with Catherine.

I mentally slapped myself. I couldn't moon over a girl, no matter how beautiful she was. I was distracted now from getting a taste of her sweetness, but I knew that this summer would be grueling. I couldn't afford to lose focus, and I was determined to make my parents proud. If my mother was going to die, the least I could give her would be honoring the tradition that had started with my great-great-grandfather. I owed her that much, and I didn't want to let her down.

First Day

Catherine

PRESENT

I drove to work for my first day. Even though my degree was in psychology, I was very grateful to get a job at a hotel in this economy. I'd abandoned my dream of pursuing astrophysics when it became clear that it wasn't a field that was welcoming to female scientists. My workplace was the most expensive hotel in my hometown, and I was really looking forward to learning the ropes.

Right after I graduated, my boyfriend, Aiden, proposed to me. All I could do was say yes. He was handsome enough. He was rich enough. And if I longed for something like what I had had with Kyle, those were stupid dreams. I still had the dreams of a teenager, and I was a young woman now. I had to be responsible and think about my future. Aiden had enough money to provide for both of us, and he told me that I didn't even need to work. However, I wanted to work. I didn't want to depend on anybody. Growing up with a single mother, I realized how important it was to maintain your independence. My mother had not dated anybody seriously while I was at home, and I was hardly going to try to rely on any man. My mother and I had done just fine without my father while he was locked up, and I intended to keep it that way. I might be getting married, but that didn't mean that I would give up my job.

Living in my hometown meant that I would run into everybody I went to high school with. I felt a sense of dread in my stomach. I didn't know if I was excited to see everybody from high school, or if I didn't want to see them. I was so naturally shy, and I was only around for senior year. Maybe they wouldn't even remember me.

I was gratified that when I walked in, all they did was hand me a packet and put me to work. I had taken a video orientation online, and I knew where everything was. I was handling things in the back office. It had nothing to do with my psychology degree, but I was happy to have a job at all. It had taken me several months to interview with a bunch of different companies, and I hadn't been able to secure a position, or even get to the final round for multiple companies. There was something missing.

Aiden bought a condo in my hometown, but he had to leave early to catch the train. I hadn't seen him this morning, although he left me a note wishing me luck.

I hoped that by hiding in the back office, I wouldn't have to run into anybody I knew.

Sam Adams

Kyle

AFTERNOON

"A Sam Adams, please." The bartender looked down his nose at me as if it was unheard of for somebody to come into this fancy hotel bar and order something that was so clearly plebeian. But he found a Sam Adams for me, and that was what mattered. I was with a bunch of my buddies, and we walked over to a table of blondes. Their tan showed that they spent all of their free time in tanning beds, and they wore too much makeup. I didn't care. Who cared how thick the icing was when the cake was all the same underneath? The only person who had been different was Catherine Jackson, and she was long gone. When she went to college, there was nobody left in this town that I cared about. Lana certainly tried to make me care, even after I left for West Point, but I couldn't get the image of Catherine out of my head.

I was no longer the boy I had been in high school, although I still had the same face. The scars were all on the inside. I had seen death in many forms. I had dealt some. I had watched my friends die around me. It made me realize how much you need to grab today. Carpe diem. When we were on leave, we grabbed girls like sailors who went on shore for the first time in seven years.

One of the girls was trying to get into my lap. I slammed a twenty down on the bar, and then I pulled her outside. I pressed her against my SUV, and she put her arms around me willingly. I was checking her tonsils when I heard someone clearing their throat.

"Excuse me, I need to get through."

When I turned around to see who had interrupted us, my jaw dropped.

Catherine was standing right there.

Too Rough

Catherine

My hands were shaking, making it hard to get the key into the lock. I got into my car, not sure that I had really seen him. Was Kyle really back in town? I had no idea. I knew that he had gone to war after graduating from West Point, but I had lost track of him.

He came up to my car window, and he knocked on it. I ignored him, just like I ignored him while he was fixing our car back in high school. I drove away, careful not to run over his feet. I looked in the rearview mirror, and I could see him standing right where I left him, a hand rubbing his jaw.

I didn't know what to do. It seemed like my default was just running away when I didn't know what I should be doing.

When I got home, Aiden was already there.

"Hey, babe. How was your first day of work?"

"It was great. I think that it's going to be a pretty simple job." I kissed him on the cheek, and he pulled me in for a harder kiss. He was a little too rough, and I pushed him away.

"Hey, don't be like that." His eyes darkened. "I just wanted to say hello to my girl."

"Just because you have a ring on my finger doesn't mean that you own me," I warned him. "I want us to take it slow and easy."

The storm clouds dispersed. "Yeah, slow and easy. That's right." He took my hand and kissed it. "How about we take it slow and easy all night?"

"No." I frowned at him. "I'm going to sleep in the basement tonight." The condo that we bought had an extra floor, which was really meant for storage. I had my college couch down there, and there was a bathroom. We could probably sublet it as an apartment, but all my stuff was there, because I didn't know what to do with it. It could go into a storage unit, but Aiden just wanted me to get rid of it.

I felt like Aiden wanted me to get rid of a lot of things. My mom had died during my sophomore year of college. I still had a lot of her stuff, stuff that Aiden didn't care about at all. She hadn't even seen me graduate, but I knew that she was proud of me. She hadn't had the same opportunity, since I had been born when she was so young.

Seeing him again woke up all of the emotions that I had buried during college. I had dated a handful of boys in college, but none of them really could hold a candle to Kyle.

What would it have been like if I had just let him catch me earlier in the year? I didn't know, and I certainly regretted running away. He had clearly expressed interest, but just like a teenager, I had ignored all the signs and thought that he was going to play me like all the rest.

Prom night was the night that I had remembered for the past few years. Aiden did not know about Kyle, and honestly, there was nothing to tell. Just one night.

I curled up in my blanket, and I fell asleep. I would never confess to Aiden, my fiancé, that I dreamed about what would have been if things had gone differently all those years ago.

DarkNet Research

Kyle

Running into Catherine again was crazy. I didn't care that the blonde I was with stalked off after I had chased Catherine. That was the girl who haunted my dreams, and somehow, she had run into me in the parking lot. Why was she at the hotel? She clearly had parked, and she seemed to be alone. Maybe she lived in town for business. In any case, I would find out.

While I was overseas, they had noticed that I had good tech skills. I had undergone extra training, the kind of training that was invaluable in a digital world.

I pulled out my smartphone, and I looked for the easy things. I found an engagement announcement. She was getting married to some guy named Aiden Gray.

There wasn't much about him online. I needed to get back to my house, so that I could use my own gear.

I drove home carefully. My parents had given me access to my trust fund when I turned eighteen. There wasn't much use for it at West Point. A lot of the other kids were twice or three times as wealthy as me.

At my house, it was totally dark and quiet. I had spent so much time in close proximity with too many other people. My home was a place where I could get away from everything. I had left the Army, but I would never forget what it had been like.

I used a retina scanner to get into my computer. I had learned the hard way that no place was really safe. Frankly, even the retina scanner wasn't foolproof. If somebody had decided to gouge out my eyeball, they could get into my computer. In fact, there were gadgets that you could use in order to mimic someone else's retina. I just had to trust that nobody with real resources would care enough to try to break into my computer.

I knew that there wasn't much information on Google about Aiden. I went to the DarkNet. I pulled all of his information, just like a creditor would. Except I needed to know even more about him.

It was strange. There wasn't much about him. The DarkNet was good at collecting information about people. There was a lot of information that was collected that people didn't know about. When the Edward Snowden revelations happened, I thought that the American people would realize just how much information the government was collecting. They had initially gotten angry, but they had gotten over it. There was actually an overwhelming sea of data about people, and I was one of the experts in the Army for data mining.

There was next to nothing on Aiden Gray. I wondered if he really existed. What if it was just an alias?

It was shady. He had never gotten a library card. He had a Social Security number, but it hadn't been used very much. Whoever this guy was, he wasn't good for Catherine.

I tapped one of my old friends, and I asked him to do a deeper look. He worked for Palantir, and he had access to things that I would never be able to touch, even with my skills. Having Top Secret clearance was awesome, though I'd just gotten a letter from the Office of Personnel Management that their database, which had security checks from people at all levels in the government, had been hacked. I had signed up for identity protection, but it had made me lose faith in the federal government's cybersecurity.

I looked for Catherine. First, I checked the hotel's database. I knew that it wasn't what most people would consider strictly legal, but she had clearly been there. I looked through the financial records of everybody who had used their credit card in the last day. She didn't appear there, under Cat or Catherine Jackson.

I searched the entire database, which took a little time. Then, I had a hit. She had just started working there. I could see from her employee file that her address wasn't too far away from the hotel.

I thought about driving there, and then I was worried that it was too far. I mean, she hadn't seen me for years. I obviously wanted to see her, but just like before, she wanted nothing to do with me. Why was she always walking in on girls kissing me? Okay, I had to admit that this time, I was an active participant.

Maybe if I went to the hotel bar again, I would see her when she left work. I thought about showing up tomorrow.

My phone buzzed, and I saw that I had a few missed calls from Lana. She must have heard that I was back in town. However, I had no idea who would even tell her. I was way out of touch with all my high school buddies, and it was only a group of casual acquaintances that had gone with me to the hotel bar to pick up girls. I realized that I needed to text them that I was gone. I figured that the girl I was with must have told them. I sent the group text anyway to tell all of them that I went home early.

Lonely

Catherine

I used to have an attentive boyfriend. I used to see him three or four times a week. Now that we lived together, Aiden spent a lot more time in his apartment in the city. I felt like he spent more nights there than he spent in our condo. I started keeping track of the nights when he was here on my calendar. There were far fewer X marks than blank spaces. He had barely come here.

I was getting lonely. I hadn't spent too much time here in high school, and I hadn't made very many female friends. The ones that had been friendly, even casually, as Adriana had been, all seemed to be gone. Not very many people came back here, it seemed. Anyway, a lot of the girls in high school had been really jealous of me. I had been surprised by it, but I was too lumpy and too ugly to be attractive, but they were still jealous because I had the attention of so many guys.

My job at the hotel was pretty simple. During the slow period, when I had nothing to do, I would read a bunch of blogs with Feedly on my phone. It was the only way that I could escape the monotony of the hotel. I was paid extremely well, though. It was as if I had a much higher skill set rather than just my psych degree. I did work that any monkey could do. I didn't need an accounting degree to check the numbers from the previous day, and I had an accounting minor. It had been brought up during my interview. While they would have preferred to pick up somebody with an actual accounting degree, most of them were too expensive, and they went to work for places like the Big 4, not ritzy hotels in medium-sized suburbs.

Before work one day, I decided to go for a run in the park next to my condo.

Running

Catherine

It felt good to pound the pavement. I realized that I had not yet worked out while being here, and I missed it. In college, everybody ran in the morning. I felt like I couldn't walk ten steps without running into somebody I knew on the trails. But in my hometown, it was totally quiet in the morning.

It was just my luck that the only other person in the park at this hour was Kyle.

"Hey there, Cat." He looked at me, from my head to my toes. "It looks like you're all hot and bothered already."

I flushed. "I'm just slightly sweaty from my run." I turned up my nose as if he didn't make me a little nervous. I began to jog faster, but he just kept pace with me. Even when I sped up a little more, he was infuriatingly fast. I started to run at my top speed, and he acted like it wasn't even hard. I eventually had to stop, because I was totally out of breath.

Kyle pulled me gently to a nearby bench. "I think that you need to sit down before you fall down."

"I have low blood pressure, and I get dizzy a lot."

"Here, have some water." I realized that he had a water pack on his back.

It felt strangely intimate to drink from his straw, but I didn't see any water fountains around.

"I'm sorry that I made you feel dizzy," he said, winking at me. "Can I walk you home? I don't want you to fall down."

I couldn't say anything without looking idiotic, so I said, "That would be wonderful." I didn't know if I would make it home on my own. I might as well accept his offer of help.

We walked slowly back to my condo, and Kyle turned to me and asked, "How is your mother?"

"My mom died a few years ago in a car accident."

"Wow, I'm so sorry. My condolences. So you are on your own?"

"No, I live with my fiancé."

I watched his jaw clench. "Fiancé?"

"Yes, I just got engaged to Aiden. We dated while I was in college, and we live together."

I was embarrassed. He probably didn't want to hear this much about my life. "Well, this one is my condo." I unlocked the door. "You can go now."

Kyle looked at me, and he looked at the door. He had promised to walk me home, and that was it. Still, he wasn't moving.

"I have to go to work soon," I hinted.

"Okay, if you ever want to see me, just call me or text me. Do you have my phone number?"

"No."

"Okay, here it is." He recited the numbers of his phone number, and I put them into my own phone. It was hard to do when my phone was strapped to my arm, but I somehow managed it.

"I'll see you soon. Call me, okay?"

"Yeah, I'll call you."

He walked away, and I went inside of my condo.

When I went into the shower, I thought about how stupid I was to try to establish any kind of relationship with him again.

I had promised myself in high school that I would stay away from Kyle, and I was breaking my promise to myself.

Just as I got out of the shower, I heard the front door open.

"Honey, I'm home."

New Wedding Planner

Catherine

I quickly threw on a dress, and then I went downstairs. Aiden wasn't alone. He had a wedding planner with him, the one that we'd talked about getting. She was impossible to book less than three years out, and I had completely despaired of reaching her. We had a list of three back-up wedding planners, and it was on my to-do list for the week to see if any of them could help with my wedding to Aiden.

"What are you doing here?"

"I thought you'd be happy," Aiden told me. "I had her agree to help us with our wedding."

"I'm so pleased to meet you," I said, turning to the wedding planner, Mrs. Chandler. "I've heard such great things about you, and I am thrilled that you have agreed to help us."

She shook my hand, and she said in a smooth voice, "I'm happy to be part of your wedding. I've been friends with Aiden's mother for many years, and I cannot wait to see how beautiful your wedding will be."

"I would love to stay and chat, but I need to go to work." I looked at the time on the microwave. "I'm going to be five minutes late as it is."

The wedding planner and Aiden looked at each other, and a moment of silent communication passed between them.

"How about this? You can call in sick, and we will work on planning the wedding. It's not like you need to work after we're married anyway. I told you you don't even need to work now."

"But I want to work. I don't think I even have sick leave yet." I tried to think back to the orientation videos. I thought that sick leave began to accrue after six months.

"I think that if you call them, they will let you take today off. Just try."

I shrugged. I went over to my cell phone, and I called into work.

"I'm sick. I will not be able to make it to work today."

"That's fine," my manager said. "Just take care. I heard that there is a nasty flu going around."

I coughed for effect. "Thank you. I'll try to rest, and I should be back tomorrow, unless it gets worse." I coughed again.

"Take all the time you need. I know that you're new, but we couldn't be more pleased to have you. You've been doing a great job so far."

I wondered how she could say that. I had been working for her for a very short time, and it seemed weird to me that she was so enthusiastic about my work. All I did was check numbers, and it wasn't like I needed to be a brain surgeon to do that.

"Why don't we all go out for brunch? We can get to know each other, and we can discuss some general ideas for the wedding; we need some kind of theme, and I think that we can figure it out if we put our heads together."

"That sounds wonderful," Mrs. Chandler said. "I will follow you there." She walked out the door, and she went towards her car.

"Shall we?" Aiden offered me his arm.

"Yes, just let me get my purse."

"You don't need it. I'm paying. Don't worry about it." He kissed my cheek.

I was worried about relying on Aiden, but surely letting him pay for the brunch with our wedding planner wasn't too bad, right?

Brunch

Catherine

He drove to the nearest breakfast place, The Pan, and we were seated almost immediately. On a weekday, it wasn't too crowded at this hour.

Our server was extremely attentive, and I already knew what I wanted. "I'll take egg whites with a side of bacon, please."

Aiden ordered Eggs Benedict, and the wedding planner ordered a fruit plate.

While we waited, the wedding planner didn't want to waste any time. "Now, let's talk about your goals for your wedding. What do you want to achieve?"

"Well, it's going to be a big event. You only get married once, you know. I want to make sure that it's memorable. I've been to way too many miserable weddings, and I want to make sure that my wedding is a lot better than those."

"And what would that mean for you?"

"Everything has to be big and beautiful."

The wedding planner turned to me. "And what do you want, my dear?"

I blinked. "Um, I guess I'll go along with what Aiden wants." I was getting overwhelmed, and we were just talking about the theme of the wedding. I would be a basket case by the time all of this was done.

"Well, what if we try to focus on the theme of winter wonderland. You wanted to have your wedding during the winter, because everybody seems to have their weddings in June. It will be easier to find the best caterers and venues if we do it during the winter."

"That sounds good to me."

I nodded. "Whatever you want, dear."

I spent the rest of brunch in a total daze, as Aiden and Mrs. Chandler discussed the particulars of the wedding. I was in completely over my head, and I had no idea how to plan a wedding. I was glad that Aiden had brought someone in, but we hadn't even set a date for our wedding. It seemed like he was going to make all the decisions by himself. And, it wasn't as if he didn't have my permission. I just had no clue how to handle all of this, and with Aiden's business sense, he certainly knew what he was doing. I got the impression from other people that the bride normally took the driver's seat when it came to wedding planning, but I was never one of those girls to dress up her dolls and dream about wedding dresses. I was more of the girl who stole other kids G.I. Joe dolls to put with my Barbies. I had no intention of getting a pretty Ken doll.

I realized, looking at Aiden, that he was more of a Ken doll, and Kyle was my G.I. Joe.

I'd never wanted someone like Aiden, but I ended up with him anyway. I was quiet as the two other people talked and talked, and I didn't see how I would possibly be part of this wedding other than being the bride. I felt like they were speaking complete gibberish, but nobody in the restaurant noticed anything weird. It was probably just me.

I had agreed to marry Aiden, but now I was regretting that decision like crazy. I had tried to push Kyle out of my mind, but that was hard now that he was here, too. I wondered what he was up to.

I didn't have an appetite, so I pushed around my food until the other two stopped.

Aiden paid the bill, and we went home.

I went upstairs to get my laptop. Aiden followed me.

"Do you have any interest in our wedding at all?" He wasn't loud, but it felt like he was yelling. He was actually more quiet than usual. "I felt like you didn't participate at all during brunch."

"I'm sure whatever you want will be fine. I mean, I have a few friends that I'm inviting, but that's it. You are the one with the most at stake, so I'm sure that you'll do a great job."

I opened my laptop to give him the hint to leave me alone. I went on Feedly to read the news.

He closed my laptop, and I jumped.

"Gosh darn it, Catherine! I'm trying to give you what you want, but you don't even care! You're so ungrateful." He was glaring at me, and I leaned back. "Do you even want to be married to me?"

I hesitated.

He covered his face with his hands. "What? We just got engaged, and you already want to back out?"

"I don't know…" I told him. "I think that getting engaged might have been a little hasty. That's all. I don't know."

"You don't know if you want to get married. I've already told the wedding planner to send Save the Date postcards to the entire list."

"You didn't ask me for my list," I told him. "Don't you need the addresses of the people that I'm inviting?"

"Yeah, yeah," he said, flapping his hand. "I'm sure that's important. Whatever."

I frowned. I felt like he didn't care about my side of the wedding at all.

"Well, if you don't feel like I'm invested in this wedding," which I wasn't, "then you can call the whole thing off. I'm sure I can find another apartment or something, and you spend all of your time in the city anyway."

"No!" he shouted. "I want you."

I cringed away from him.

Abruptly, he straightened up and touched his tie. "I'm sorry. That was unacceptable. A gentleman doesn't yell at his lady. Of course we'll send postcards to your side of the wedding. I can forward Mrs. Chandler's introductory email to you, and you can email her whatever information you think she needs."

I felt out of the loop. Mrs. Chandler had sent an introductory email? She hadn't sent it to me, obviously. I wondered if I was just going to be out of the loop for the entire wedding. Today, that was by choice. But obviously Aiden had a lot more going on than what I was seeing. It was like he was a glacier, and all I could see were the parts above the water.

New Evidence

Kyle

My phone dinged as I got an email from my VIP list. I opened my new email and I frowned.

My friend had dug up dirt on Aiden Gray, and it didn't look so good. For one thing, he had definitely blackmailed Catherine's boss into hiring her. He had embarrassing videos of her boss in flagrante delicto. As soon as Catherine had expressed the desire to go home, he had figured out a way for her to have a cushy, minimally demanding job so that she could spend most of her time on him.

I also had a record of every time that he used a toll road. He didn't come home to her all that often, just two or three times a week, sometimes less. He spent most of his time in the city, and I didn't know how I felt about that.

I loved that Catherine was alone and basically free for the taking. I hated that she was engaged to a douchebag. She deserved better. Heck, I wasn't good enough for her, but I was way better than Aiden Gray, that was for sure. He was a scumbag, and my friend wasn't even done digging up dirt. Those were just the preliminary findings. Who knew what his real name was?

I knew that I could go to Catherine with this stuff, but there was no guarantee that she'd believe me. I was a guy that she had slept with once years ago. He was her fiancé.

My phone buzzed again, but I ignored it after I saw who it was. It was Lana, and I hoped that she would get the message after I didn't answer her messages.

I hadn't seen any of my other ex-girlfriends since I had been in town, and even if I had, they wouldn't be as persistent as Lana. She wanted me, for seemingly no reason at all. I couldn't understand her, but then, it was a path to madness to try to understand women. They made no sense at all.

I needed to go for a run or grab a drink. Since I had run pretty recently, I decided to take the unhealthy option.

I went back to that hotel bar. Who even knew if I would see Catherine again...

As soon as I walked into the room, I could feel that she was there. I swung my head around to look for her, and she was right there, in the corner of the bar all by herself.

"Sam Adams," I told the bartender, who gave me the same nasty look as before. Hey, I was a paying customer.

"Watch yourself."

I blinked. I guessed the bartender was pretty protective. She had two empty glasses in front of her, so I guessed that the bartender oversupplied her with alcohol in order to feel like he was doing a great job.

I touched Catherine's hand. "Hey, how are you?"

She turned to me, and I thought that her eyes were red. I had a strange sense of deja vu.

"What's wrong?" Why had she been crying?

"Oh, it's nothing."

"It obviously is something, if you're crying and in a bar. Come on, tell me what's bothering you."

"I don't know if I want to get married. Aiden surprised me with a wedding planner this morning, and I had to call in sick so that we could do a lot of planning." She blurted out her story, and then she looked at the bartender. "You didn't hear that."

"I didn't hear anything. I am basically mute. Don't worry, I cannot hear anything coming out of your mouth right now."

"Good." I nodded. "Make sure that it stays that way." If looks could kill, the bartender would've killed me on the spot. I only smiled. He had no idea who he was dealing with. He was soft, and I was still hard from coming back from the war. Most Americans lived quiet lives, and they didn't realize how much they owed people who were risking their lives every day. I lost a lot of good people in the sandbox, and I had nightmares still about the times when I heard a bomb going off and had not known if I was going to live or die.

Bartender

Catherine

I smiled as Jack, the bartender, gave Kyle a fierce glare. "I don't take orders from scruffy ruffians, no matter how handsome." Jack was gay, and he was a quick friend the first time that I met him. It wasn't as if we were close, but we were certainly friendly.

"Were you drinking alone?" Kyle turned away from Jack. I think that he didn't consider Jack a threat, and Kyle's gaydar must've been pretty strong.

"I don't know."

"Well, too lonely to drink alone. I'll buy you a drink. Heck, I will pay your tab."

"That's very kind of you, but I can't imagine that I can accept it. I have my own money now. I can pay for my own drinks, and I get a discount for being an employee anyways. I should be paying for your drink."

"Nonsense. I won't hear of it."
He took out his credit card and put
it on the counter. He motioned at
Jack. "Please just charge the card
whenever we are done for the
night, okay?"

From the look in Jack's eyes, I
guessed that he would charge it as
much as he could. He sometimes
made people give him one hundred
percent tips when they gave him
their cards, and I had a feeling that
tonight was going to be one of
those times.

"Now, why are you so upset?"

"I'm just not sure that I should have said yes to Aiden. He put a bunch of pressure on me to do it, and I just don't know if it was the right decision."

"Well, do you love him? I feel like marriage should be between a man and a woman who love each other. Or a man and a man who love each other. Just two people who love each other."

"I have no idea." I shrugged and shook my head. "What is love?"

"Baby, don't hurt me." I smiled at him. He grinned back.

"If you loved him, you'd probably know it, right? Isn't it something like, 'They say you know when you know. I don't know...'"

"Look at you, quoting Katy Perry at me. I didn't know that you knew her songs."

"Shh. It's a secret." He winked at me, and I could feel myself getting wet. I was surprised by his secret love of Katy Perry, but somehow it made him more likable.

"Yeah, I mean…it seemed like a good idea at the time. But the closer we get to the wedding, the less I want to do it. I mean, Aiden just sent out a million invitations to his side and didn't even ask me whom I wanted to invite. Technically, half of this wedding should be mine…but I just can't take an interest in it."

"That's probably a sign that you shouldn't go through with it. And I'm not even saying that as someone who has an interest in you. I'm just saying it as someone who…"

"Wait, what? You have an interest in me? Is that present tense?" I slurred my words a little bit, and I was surprised to find that I was hiccuping. Who knew how many drinks I'd had... That bartender Jack really didn't want to do his job. I could see a bunch of empty bottles near me, and I covered my mouth as I hiccuped again.

"Focus on the matter at hand. We can talk about that later," Kyle said, eyeing the bartender who was drifting close to us. "Hey, man, can we get rid of all of the empties, please?"

"Hey, I've been keeping them coming." I saw him swipe the card again, and I saw that he keyed in 3 digits as the tip. Kyle was going to get a surprise, but that was a good lesson to learn. You never just give someone your credit card and tell them to run wild with it. Jack could definitely do a lot worse, and still Kyle would have a lesson he'd never forget.

"I've never forgotten you." It was like in *Mean Girls* when Lindsay Lohan talks about having word vomit. I was so drunk that I could barely differentiate between my thoughts and my words. Okay, I couldn't differentiate between them at all.

"Really?"

"I don't think I love him. I think I love you."

Just then, Kyle's phone rang. I saw the caller ID flash. *Lana*, it said, and there was a picture of Lana in a wet, white bikini. It was basically transparent, and I could see the outline of her areola.

I reeled back as if someone had slapped me. What was I doing in a bar with Kyle, the notorious womanizer? Hadn't I just caught him making out with another girl? I felt like I was too stupid to learn. I knew that girls flocked around him, and I always thought that I was different...that I wasn't like the rest. But I was just a game to him, and I needed to get out of here.

Throwing My Ring

Catherine

"Jack," I called, "can you call a cab?" Thanks to my salary, I didn't need to count pennies anymore. My tuition and board were paid for, but I still had to buy my own computer, textbooks, and assorted fees. During college, I'd kept a big coin jar. Whenever I ran out of money, I'd pick out the quarters. There were a lot of times when I didn't have any quarters in that big jar. Or dimes. Or heck, nickels. It had been a long road to get through my degree in psychology, but I'd made it through somehow, even after my mother died.

Jack nodded, and he just picked up the phone to call the concierge.

I slapped Kyle on the arm. I must have done it too hard, though, because he winced a little bit. "Thanks for the drinks, Kyle."

"No! Wait! There's more."

"What's more?" I blinked slowly.

"I have to tell you about your scumbag fiancé."

"What about him? He's not a scumbag...just a little insensitive."

Kyle leaned down, and I turned my mouth to catch his. He wasn't aiming for my mouth, though. He whispered in my ear.

"He got you your job."

"What?" I didn't think that my ears were working right. The whole room was moving a little bit around me.

"He has dirt on your manager. He blackmailed her to get her to do what he wanted. I'm sorry, Catherine. I know how independent you are."

I started crying, and he looked alarmed. Jack put a stack of napkins near mc.

"Thanks, Jack. You've earned your tips." Kyle frowned.

"What?"

"Shut up. You're the douchebag. You left me all those years ago. The military was more important for you."

"I wanted you," Kyle told me. "I wanted it to work out. You spent an entire year avoiding me...I didn't think that you were interested."

"I don't think that it does any good now," I slurred. "You have a million girlfriends, and I'm about to get married to that douchebag. Who cares? Does it matter?"

I walked away, feeling loose and floaty. He didn't follow me. I was aware that I wasn't walking in a straight line. Good thing that I lived so close. Was my car here or at home? If it was here, I'd have to figure out a way to get back. That was a problem for another time.

When I got to the front, there was a cab waiting for me. I swallowed, feeling all of that alcohol coming up and burning my throat. I gave the driver my address, and he quickly punched it into his GPS.

We drove all the way home, and I took the time to think about what Kyle had told me. Was it true? Had I gotten this job because of Aiden?

But then again, could I really trust the word of a womanizer like Kyle? For goodness' sake, he had a nearly naked picture of Lana on his phone — not hidden away like a secret, but right there in the caller ID. He acted like she wasn't important, but she was clearly still part of his life. I didn't know where I fit in, but he had a million people trying to be his girlfriend, and I didn't want to get into a knife fight. I knew from experience that Lana was a dirty fighter, and she had no love for me.

I stumbled into the house. Aiden was home for once, drinking a fifth of whiskey straight from the bottle.

"You're home late."

"I'm fine," I said. "I think that I've drunk less than you. Wasn't that bottle full this morning?"

He shrugged. "I hold my liquor better than you do."

That was true. I struggled to get my shoes off, and I carried them into my room before flinging them onto my shoe rack. No matter how drunk I got, I needed to take care of my shoes. It was strange how it focused me to think about them.

I took off my dress, and I put on comfortable sweats and a t-shirt.

All that alcohol was wearing off, and I stopped feeling as if I would vomit any second. I lay down so that the room would stop spinning around me. Was it true that Aiden had pulled strings for me to get my job? Suddenly, it seemed like the most important question in the world.

I used the wall for support, one hand lightly trailing on it, and I walked to the living room, where Aiden was still drinking and texting furiously on his phone.

"Who are you talking to?"

"Nobody." He pressed the button to make the screen go dark. It buzzed again, and I saw a picture of a blonde girl come up.

"Who's she?"

"Just a girl at work." He looked at me. "You're obviously wasted. You better go to bed."

"Don't patronize me," I slurred at him. "You have a lot to answer for, buddy."

He shook his head. "I don't think is the right time for this conversation."

"When is the right time?" I started crying, and I wasn't even that ashamed. It felt good to let some of this out. "When is the right time to talk about this? You're never here."

"Sure, if you want to talk about this now, we'll talk. You want to know whom I've been contacting? It's Natalia. She's an assistant at the office, and she gives great head."

I was confused. "What?" I pulled at my earlobe. "Do you mean that she's good at getting ahead?"

"No, I mean, I'm sleeping with her more than I'm sleeping with you. You don't want to have sex, and that's fine in a wife. My dad had a girl in the city, and my mom raised me in the suburbs throughout my own childhood. I have no reservations about following in his footsteps."

I blinked and then blinked again. "So what you're saying is, you're cheating on me with someone from work, and you expect me to have and raise your kids no matter what?"

"Yes."

"And the job that I have now..."

"You have that job completely due to my influence. I have incriminating evidence of your manager, and your manager jumps when I say so."

This seemed wrong to me, but I wasn't sure why. I just felt my shoulders tense up.

"Keep the ring. I don't think this is going to work." It took me several tries, but I pulled the ring off of my finger and threw it at him.

I grabbed my purse and walked out of the house. I hoped that policemen patrolled the park at night, because that's where I was heading. I checked my parking spot, and my car wasn't there. I must have left my car at the hotel.

Late Run

Kyle

I woke up sweating. I looked around me. I was in a tranquil bedroom in my own house in America, not sleep deprived in a sandbox.

I tore off the covers, and I did the only thing that could drive the nightmares away: exhaust myself to sleep.

I put on a shirt over my sweats, and I picked up my iPod. I put on my sneakers, and I went out to the park.

When I got there, I thought that I was hallucinating.

"Catherine?"

I saw her turn around. Like me, she was dressed in sweats and a t-shirt. Unlike me, she still seemed inebriated.

"Kyle..." she said as she drifted towards me. "What are you doing here?"

"I couldn't sleep. What's the matter? Have you been crying?"

That was a stupid question. I could see the tear tracks on her face in the light from the lamp posts.

"Aiden said it's all true...and he has another girl in the city."

My report hadn't told me that, but it wasn't a surprise, considering how few nights he spent with Catherine. "Oh."

"Why are men like this?" she sobbed. "Why don't men ever want to be faithful?"

"Here, let's sit down on this bench." I could see a cop pass us by, giving us side-eye.

"Why do all men suck?"

"Hey, not all men suck. Just some of us." I winked at her, but she didn't smile.

"I just want to fall in love with someone who loves me back."

"I love you," I told her. My heart beat fast after I confessed it.

She obviously didn't care. "Sure you do. Just like Aiden does. Pfft." Despite her harsh words, she spun so that her head was in my lap. I tried to roll her down my thighs, away from my erection, but it just made her crawl towards it. I tried to breathe slow so that she wouldn't notice it sticking out in front of her.

She nuzzled my thigh the way that I would bury my face in a pillow. It was a form of sweet torture to feel her touching me. One, I'd dreamed about this girl and her scent for years, so it was so good. Two, I had an erection, and she thought that all men, including me, were scum.

I started braiding her hair.

"That feels nice," she sighed. "When did you learn to braid hair?"

"I can crochet, too." I smiled.

"Why?"

"My mom wanted a girl. She used to braid my hair. She kept it kind of long when I was a little kid. She said that the Scots had braided their hair, so my dad let her. It didn't make me too girly."

Catherine turned and smiled at me, and it was like being hit by a ray of sunlight. "That's funny."

"A little, I guess." I traced the tip of her nose.

"Don't touch it. It's ugly." She clamped a hand over her nose.

"I think that every inch of you is beautiful." I tugged her hand away. "Never hide yourself."

"I'm too lumpy, and my nose is too long. Guys like women with boobs like Lana."

I coughed. "Well, that's true for certain kinds of men."

"Including you."

"Maybe when I was younger." I kept braiding her hair. "But now...I know that I want to spend time with women who are beautiful on the inside. I'm not talking just about romantic relationships. I want to have deeper relationships, not go off into a bathroom somewhere and come out a few minutes later, you know?"

"I don't know," she said softly. "I've never had that kind of relationship."

"It's not a relationship. It's not even a one night stand. It's just two ships bumping hulls for a few minutes. And then she goes and finds someone else and does it all again."

"It's like you are another species. I can't imagine doing anything like that."

I shrugged, though she had closed her eyes and couldn't see me. "It's life for some people. It's been my life. If I found the right woman, I'd stop."

"Well, let me know when you've found her."

There was a beat of silence, and then I confessed, "I already have." I'd just told her that I loved her, and she was still surprised. It was probably the alcohol.

She was totally still in my lap. I didn't want to scare her, especially when she was so emotionally devastated by Aiden's confession. "What?"

"It's you," I told her softly, stroking her braided hair. "It's always been you."

I bent down and touched her mouth with my own. She tasted sweet, like peppermint candy. It was such an uncomfortable position to kiss her in, though, and I broke the kiss after only a moment.

"Wow." Catherine sat up. "I guess the chemistry isn't gone."

"Yeah, it's definitely still there."

She looked at my lap for the first time. "Wow, how did I not notice that?"

I shrugged. "It's not important."

"That's such a refreshing change. Aiden always seemed to want sex whenever he wanted it, but never when I did. He was so pushy."

"I promise you that if we were together, I'd never pressure you to have sex when you didn't want it."

"I don't know." She folded her hands in her lap and looked down. "I just broke up with Aiden. I don't think that I should get involved with anybody else. But I have nowhere to go — the condo is Aiden's."

"That's okay," I said. "I'll take you home."

"I just told you that I shouldn't get involved with anybody else...that sounds like I'd be getting really involved with you."

"Nah, I meant my parents' home," I corrected her quickly. "Believe me, they'd love to have some company...especially beautiful company like you who would draw me in like a moth to a flame."

She smiled at me, and my heart broke a little bit for this extraordinarily beautiful girl who, through no fault of her own, had needed to guard herself, only to be stabbed in the heart by a scumbag. I swore to myself that I would never treat her that way.

"I'd like that."

"Come on," I said, standing up and dusting off my jeans. "Let's go to my car."

I walked slowly to my own home with her. It wasn't big, but it was a good fixer-upper. I would put it back on the market once I had the time to do all the home improvement projects that I wanted to do. For now, though, it was home.

"This seems nice," she said, after I unlocked the door and brought her inside. She looked at my leather couch.

"It's all of my mom's discarded furniture," I told her. "She redecorates constantly, and she doesn't have any use for all of this stuff. She'd donate it, but she said she'd give me anything that I wanted."

Catherine walked around inside of my home, and it struck me how right she looked inside of it.

"Come to my garage," I told her. "I'll give you the full tour one day, but I'd like to go to sleep tonight."

"Oh, yes, of course," she said, a blush creeping up her cheeks. "I'm sorry."

"Don't be," I said, smiling. "I want to help you, but it's the dead of night. I think my mom might still be awake, but we need to hurry to catch her. I don't want to wake her up."

She got into the passenger side of my car, and I backed out of my garage. We drove quickly to my parents' house. The light in the kitchen was still on, and I could hear my mom singing as she washed the dishes.

"Come on in," I said, turning. She was staring at the house. "It's not that big."

"It's huge!"

"Come on!" I said, pulling her a little bit. "It's not a big deal."

I used the keypad to open the kitchen door. "Hey, Mom!"

She spun around, a soapy hand on her heart, a circle of wetness spreading on her shirt. "My goodness, Kyle! You scared me half to death! Couldn't you have called before you showed up? You're welcome anytime, of course, but a little warning would be nice."

"Sorry, Mom." I walked over and bent to drop a kiss on her cheek. "I brought a guest for you. She needs a place to sleep, and she'd feel more comfortable if she weren't staying at my place."

My mom looked at Catherine. She noticed the red eyes and the way Catherine was sniffling. "Of course. We can put her in your room. The guest bedroom is full of my crafting supplies. Do you have a suitcase?"

No Suitcase

Catherine

"No," I whispered. "I don't have a suitcase."

"Well, let me see if I have some clothes that would fit you." She looked me up and down. "You're not my size ...I think I might need to raid my husband's closet. Maybe you should use Kyle's old clothes from high school. I think that some of the small shirts would be just a bit baggy, and that's good enough for now."

Kyle, his mom, and I went upstairs. She flicked on the lights, and I liked the mezzanine that they had. I went into Kyle's room. It had a bunch of sports posters everywhere, and it smelled like a boy.

His mom sniffed. "It still smells like sweaty socks in here. Boys." She shook her head. "My bedroom is the same way, if you can believe it."

I smiled. "I'm so grateful that you're even letting me stay in your home. I don't mind."

"Well, let me get some Oust! and then we'll spray it around so that you don't have to smell all of this."

"I'm allergic to Oust!, but don't worry. I have lived in smellier conditions, I promise."

She opened the bathroom door, and I saw that it was small but fine. "Okay, if you want to take a shower, you just have to flip this switch."

"You have a tankless water heater right here?"

"Yes, we do. We had a boiler, but Kyle here liked to take long showers, and so we had to switch it up." Even though her words were exasperated, she was grinning.

"It was a great project, Mom. It taught me all about plumbing and gave me plenty of manly bonding time with my dad."

She nodded. "It did. And it meant that I didn't have to make sure to shower before you." She looked at me. "He would take these long showers at the end of the day, and when I showered, I only got huge amounts of cold water. So we had to do something, you see." She waved her hand. "But enough about me. I'm sure you are tired. We'll let you get settled in. There are spare toothbrushes from the dentist in the right-hand drawer under his sink. Do you like pancakes?"

I blinked at the extremely abrupt change in subject. "Yes?"

"Okay, I'll cook you some blueberry pancakes tomorrow, then. Sleep tight, Catherine." She shooed Kyle out of his own room, and she closed the door. I looked around. This room was frankly nicer than my own. I took a quick shower and brushed my teeth, and then I stole a huge shirt from his closet. It smelled like him, and I fell asleep dreaming that I was engulfed in his arms.

Bacon, Eggs, and Blueberry Pancakes

Catherine

When I woke up, I could smell bacon. I went to the bathroom and quickly washed my face. I put on my clothes from yesterday, crumpled from the park. I made a face, but it was the best I could do under the circumstances.

"Hey, Catherine!" His mom was way too cheerful in the morning. "I made pancakes, bacon, and eggs. Do you like maple syrup or blueberry syrup better?"

"Um, I've never had blueberry syrup on pancakes."

"Blueberry syrup it is, then. I buy it from a farmer who makes his own, and boy, is it good! Way better than store-bought stuff." She plunked down a container of syrup, and she quickly gave me a huge stack of pancakes.

"I can't eat this much." I stared at it. It looked like enough food to feed me for a week.

"Nonsense! Breakfast is the most important meal of the day. If you want, I can put it into a Tupperware container once you're full."

"Okay," I told her. I drizzled syrup all over it, and I took my first bite. The pancakes were soft and tender, and I loved them so much.

I swallowed. "Wow, these are so good."

"Better than your mom makes, hmm?"

I looked down at my pancakes. "My mom is dead."

"Oh, I'm so sorry! I always put my foot in my mouth."

"No, no, it's okay." I smiled at her. "It's been a few years. She never made me pancakes, though. She was always too busy."

"Well, let me give you a mom hug." She hugged me. "And you can have more pancakes if you want. Kyle's father isn't up yet, that lazy man, and so I still have an enormous quantity of batter sitting by the side."

"I'm pretty sure that I won't need any more pancakes, but that's very generous of you." I smiled at her. She was so bright and happy that it was impossible to be blue around her. I knew that she was a cancer survivor, but she was relentlessly cheerful.

I ate my pancakes, and she gave me a plate of eggs and bacon. Either of the plates would be twice the normal breakfast for me, but I tried to eat it all to be polite. She was an excellent cook.

"What's in the eggs?" They tasted different.

"Soy sauce."

"What?"

"Soy sauce. It gives the eggs a slightly different texture, and it makes them salty. Better than salt and pepper, am I right?"

"Wow, I've never eaten eggs with soy sauce in them before."

"I dated a Vietnamese guy once, and he ate his eggs with soy sauce in the morning. I broke up with him, obviously, but the habit stuck. Once you try soy sauce with your eggs, you just don't go back to plain old salt and pepper."

I nodded. "Yeah, I can see that."

I finished up my food, and Kyle's dad still hadn't come downstairs. Mrs. Richards turned off the stove, and she told me, "I'm going to help you go back to your house and pick up your things. Kyle said you might need a hand."

"Oh, that's okay," I said bashfully, ducking my head. "I don't want to put you through any trouble. I can call a taxi."

"No! I won't hear of it. I'm a housewife, and I certainly have the time to pick up your things. You can stay here until you find another place. No trouble at all." She leaned in conspiratorially. "I'll cook you pancakes every day until you find a new apartment."

I smiled at her. "With your pancakes, I'd never leave!"

She laughed. "You're such a sweet girl. Come on, now. Just leave those dishes in the sink, and we'll go get your stuff."

I realized, as I cleared my plates and put them in the sink, that she had an iron will. She hid it well in a light glove, but this woman was used to getting her way. If she were a man, she would be a five-star general. It was fortunate for America's enemies that this woman wasn't in the military, because they would need to run.

I gave her the directions to my place by punching it into her GPS, and we listened to some oldies on the radio.

When we got to my house, all of my stuff was shredded and outside. It must have rained last night, because all of it was wet and soggy.

My landlady was out front. I got out of the car.

"This is a disgrace! Are you on drugs? Did you do all of this while you were hallucinating?" The landlady came to me and shook her finger in my face. "I won't rent to anybody who does drugs. You need to get rid of this immediately."

"Now, wait a minute," Mrs. Richards said soothingly, trying to smooth her ruffled feathers. "This young lady has been at my house all night. She has nothing to do with this. We can get this cleared out, but..."

"I don't care where she's been all night. Stuff like this drives down the property value and the rent. I want this to be cleaned up immediately."

I wiped away a tear. "Yes, ma'am."

When I agreed while crying, she ran out of steam. "Good." She turned around and walked into her own condo.

I started to cry more, and I went to survey the damage. It looked like everything I owned was out on this lawn. I had pictures of me and my mother, and the glass in the frames had punctured the pictures beyond saving. I cried, holding the pieces of the frames together. How could Aiden do this to me?

"Is that your mama?"

I nodded. "Yes, she is."

"She's pretty, just like you. Listen, sweetheart, how about this? I'll hire some large men to help clean this all up, and I'll take you home. We can watch a movie."

"But I need to clean it up."

"It'll be cleaned up," she told me firmly. "But you're in no state to deal with this incredible mess, and I'm not going to stand and watch you cry as you gather up your possessions. It's too painful. So for my sake, please come with me."

"I don't know if I can afford to hire anybody. I'm homeless."

"Honey, I'll take care of it. And you are not homeless. You're with me."

Mermaid Blanket

Kyle

I was angry enough to kill. After work, I immediately drove to my parents' house. My mom had texted me to ask if I would come over. She'd given Catherine a lot of Swiss chocolate, but she thought that she would do better if I came by.

I walked into the den, and Catherine was curled up in one of Mom's silly mermaid blankets, watching *Pride and Prejudice.*

I got a lot gentler when I sat next to her. "Hey." I leaned in and hugged her.

She gave me a fragile smile. "Hi."

"How are you doing?"

"I don't know. I don't know if I have a job. I just started...who knows if I'll get a paycheck?"

"We'll figure something out, don't worry." I took her hand. "We can do it together. I can make the son of a gun pay."

"Don't," she said, staring straight at me. "I'm better off without him, and you know it. Your dad said that we should sue him for destruction of property, and we're going to look into it. It's better if we settle this legally, you know?"

I flexed my shoulders. "That's okay for now. But if you want me to beat him up for you, just say the word."

"Thank you." She wiggled out of the mermaid blanket, and she leaned in for a kiss.

I kissed her soft and slow, but she didn't want a soft kiss. She climbed on top of me, and I felt myself getting hard. "I don't want to do it in your parents' house. Take me home."

She didn't need to tell me twice.

A Pirate's Captive

Kyle

I picked her up, and I slung her over my shoulder, like I was a pirate and she was my captive.

"Bye, Mom," I called as I went through the kitchen. Mom was throwing things into her crockpot, and she just smiled and waved as she watched me take Catherine out of the house, as if it happened every day. Mom took everything in stride.

I put Catherine into my passenger seat, and then I drove fast enough to get a ticket. Somebody upstairs must have been smiling on me and what we were about to do, because I got green lights all the way home.

I pulled Catherine into my bedroom. "I guess today isn't the day for that tour, either." I took off her shirt, and I whistled softly. Her body had only gotten better in the years since high school. She'd packed on some curves, and I appreciated them. I touched her breast gently. "Wow."

"You like it? I know I'm fatter than last time..."

"Fatter? More womanly. And you're still so hot..."

"Thanks." She hugged herself.

"Take off your pants," I commanded softly.

She stared into my eyes, and as if hypnotized, she pulled down her pants. I could see that she was wearing plain underwear, and it just turned me on more. If she had been wearing lace, I would've known that she had dressed for Aiden when she left her condo. Knowing that she was still so innocent made me want her more.

I ripped off my clothes, and I threw them on the ground. I pulled her into my arms, and then I fell back on the bed with her on top of me. We dry humped with her underwear still on, and it was better and more intense than full sex with other women. She kissed me again and again, and then I broke the kiss.

She gasped when I bit her breast, and I rubbed her clit with one of my hands. She writhed on top of me, so I pulled the crotch of her panties to the side.

"Are you on birth control?"

"Yes," she whispered.

That was enough for me to plunge into her. I'd been waiting for too long to wait for her to undress now.

She felt like heaven. She felt like coming home. She felt like a perfect velvet glove, encasing my erection. I wouldn't last long like this, and I paid special attention to her clit. Ladies always came first.

She shuddered through an orgasm on top of me, and I couldn't hold on when her body clenched around mine. I gritted my teeth as I released inside of her.

"That was amazing," she said. "I've never had sex like that with anybody but you."

"Same here," I said, kissing her cheek. "You're the best I've ever had."

"You're not just saying that?"

"No. I wouldn't say it if I didn't mean it."

She kissed me, and we fell asleep. I was dimly aware that I needed to wash, but nothing could have convinced me to get out of that bed when Catherine was in my arms. Not even a bomb.

For the first time since I left the military, I slept through the night.

* * *

I had a stupid grin on my face for the entirety of the next day. I was working on some bookkeeping for my dad's business. I hadn't found a full-time position yet, and my dad was willing to pay me a salary to work whenever I wanted. It wasn't the best thing that I could be doing, but it wasn't the worst, either.

I saw everybody in the shop stop working. I stood up. What was going on?

I got out of the office, and I saw Lana.

She was wearing some kind of leather bodysuit, like a BDSM fantasy. She was wearing thigh-high boots, and she caught every eye in the shop. She looked like a wet dream. Someone else's wet dream.

"What do you want?" I said. "Everybody, get back to work."

She followed me into the office.

Towel

Catherine

Kyle had driven me back to his parents' house in the morning, because I still had some salvageable clothes that had been through the dryer. They were still okay, and I preferred to wear my own clothes as opposed to his.

I was surprised to find that Kyle's mother had already gotten my car back from the hotel. She handed me the keys when I got back to the house. "Not that I mind driving you around, honey, but I thought that you'd appreciate your own set of wheels."

"Thank you, ma'am."

"Oh, honey, you don't have to thank me! It was a pleasure. You can stay here as long as you want. Living in a house with two boys, I really appreciate having a little more estrogen around." She kissed my cheek. "And I think that you might want to visit someone who doesn't live here..."

"I'll go over to Kyle's house now to surprise him." I smiled at her. She knew what I wanted. Whom I wanted. "I'll be back later."

"Honey, if you come back tomorrow, I won't be surprised or offended." She winked at me. It was weird, because she was his mom, but at the same time it felt good to know that she approved of me and Kyle.

I went to his house and I rang the doorbell.

The front door opened almost instantly.

A mostly naked girl answered the door wearing just a towel.

I felt like the wind had been knocked out of me. I tried to control my breathing, but I couldn't. "What are you doing here?"

The woman in front of me was the kind of girl that you would see on the front of magazines. "Hello, I'm Lana. I'm Kyle's girlfriend."

I vaguely remembered that years ago, he had been involved with her. I thought that he had a sexy picture of her on his phone. And now, looking at her perfect body clad only in a towel, I could see the appeal. I had a few extra pounds, and she clearly had none.

"I'm sorry for disturbing you." I turned and I left. I heard the door shut behind me, and I tried to hold back my tears. What was going on?

I got into my car, and I drove back home to Kyle's parents' house. I didn't know what was going on, and I had no idea why he had me staying with his parents while he had another woman staying in his house, but I didn't really want to stick around to find out.

He was such a player when we were younger, and it was obvious that he had continued to be a player until now. Hadn't I just found him making out in the parking lot with a girl? I was so stupid for testing somebody who had proven time and time again that he believed that women were as disposable as Kleenex.

My eyes were filled with tears. I couldn't go back to Kyle's house, and I didn't want to see his parents right now. So I went and I drove around town. I had nowhere to go. After Aiden had cheated on me, and Kyle obviously was the same kind of guy, I really questioned my own judgment. Why did I have a habit of falling in love with the worst guys? Was it something about me that just said that I was a magnet for guys who would use and lose me?

I was crying so much that I didn't realize that the light I was going through was red. It was a surprise when a small Volkswagen came out of nowhere, and my car protected me from the worst of the impact. I was knocked unconscious as metal crunched and glass shattered around me.

Lana Twice

Kyle

When I was done with work, I took a cold beer out of the refrigerator. I had definitely earned it. Last night, I had to let Lana spend the night in my house. I felt bad because she came all the way from out of state to convince me to get back together with her. It had been an hour-long discussion, and she hadn't wanted to let the subject drop, although I made it crystal clear that there was somebody else already in my life. I didn't remember if she remembered what prom night had been like, but I didn't tell her all about Catherine.

Last night, I told her that she should leave by the time I came home from work. I had made toast for her, and I left strawberry jam next to it. I remembered that, years ago, her lips had always tasted like strawberries, so I guessed that she liked them.

I didn't know why Lana made the effort to come all the way back home just to see me. She could have saved herself a lot of time and effort if she had just called. I wondered if she still had my phone number. Maybe she didn't.

After I was done with my beer, I tossed it into the recycling bin, and I drove home. When I got out of my car, Lana came to meet me.

"What are you doing here? I thought that you left this morning."

"Is that any way to greet someone? Particularly somebody who has been your friend for so long?" Lana pouted, but I was not falling for her act. She looked like a cat who got the cream, and I wanted to know why.

"What did you do today? I expected you to leave this morning, right after I went to work."

"I wanted to talk some more. I think I can change your mind."

I looked at her outfit. It was skin-tight, the kind of thing that you saw girls wearing at nightclubs. At another time, in another place, I would accept the invitation that she was issuing, but I had no interest right now. I was getting more serious with Catherine, and I didn't want to mess it up.

"Let's talk inside." I went into my living room and sat on the couch.

Lana jumped into my lap. She ground on my body like a stripper, and I was not impressed. "Cut it out, Lana." I gently pushed her away, but she fought it, clinging to me with her thighs just like clamps.

After I lifted her off of me, she said, "Come on. You know that we're good together."

I snorted. "Lana, it's been over forever."

Lana pouted. "What? Do you think I'm ugly?"

"Of course you aren't, but just being pretty doesn't mean that you can have whatever you want."

She looked down. "I guess."

"Listen, how about we order some pizza and just kick back and watch a movie like old friends?"

She wrinkled her nose. "I don't eat pizza. I'm vegan."

"We can get it without cheese if you want." Please don't take me up on this offer. Pizza without cheese is just bread with vegetables on it.

"Nah, pizza is way too fattening. I don't eat gluten, either."

"They've got gluten-free crusts..." And they tasted like cardboard but had the strength of paper.

"No, that's fine. I can get out of your hair."

I tried to hide my obvious relief, but Lana caught it.

"Expecting someone tonight?" She arched one brow in a way that I used to find sexy a long time ago.

"My girlfriend, Catherine. She and I are getting more serious…and I'm guessing that she'll come over tonight. In fact," I said, checking my watch, "she should be here right now."

Lana smirked a little, and that small action set off alarm bells. "I might know something about it."

"What did you do?"

"You sure you don't want to get back together?"

"One hundred percent."

Lana looked down at her hands. "She came by earlier. I'd just gotten out of the shower, and..."

"Oh no."

"Yeah, I answered the door in a towel. And I might have..."

"What did you say?"

"I told her that we were involved."

All the color drained out of my face. "No, you didn't."

She bit her lip. "I did."

I didn't even have the time to chew Lana out for scaring Catherine off. After Aiden's insanity, I knew that Catherine was a little gun-shy to begin with. I needed to talk to her.

Now.

I yanked my cell phone out, and I pulled up my Favorites list. Her phone rang once, twice, but she didn't answer.

"She's not picking up." I tried to keep my panic out of my voice, but it was as plain as the nose on my face.

"Try again. I'm sure she's running around, trying to find her phone." Lana had a strand of hair around one finger, and she was biting her nails. I thought that she felt bad about what she had done, but I had more important things to worry about.

On the second ring, someone picked up.

"Catherine! Oh my goodness, I need to talk to you."

"Do you know Catherine, sir?" The voice on the other end of the line was about an octave lower than Catherine's voice.

"Who is this?"

"I'm Dr. Roberts. If you're close to Catherine, you should come to the hospital. Her condition is critical. Do you have the contact information for any of her family members?"

"I'm her fiancé," I lied. If she'd let me put a ring on her finger, I definitely would. "Her parents are gone, and she doesn't have any siblings."

"That'll do. Do you have a name?"

"Kyle Richards."

"I'll leave a note in the patient's file about you. You should come as quickly as you can. She may not have long to live."

The doctor hung up. I sat there, immobile, for a few seconds. Catherine couldn't die. She just couldn't. There was too much left for us to do. We weren't even married, and we might be out of time right now.

Something inside of me came roaring to life. It simply wasn't fair for Catherine to be fighting for her life, and if she died before I could set the record straight, I'd never forgive myself or Lana. There was too much of our story that hadn't been told.

Dreaming of Kyle

Catherine

I was having a nice dream.

In it, Kyle was holding me in his arms. I felt the heavy weight of his arm on my rib cage. I felt the hard planes of his chest against my back and the tiny abrasion of his facial hair against my neck. We had one night together, but I had never forgotten it. I'd had other partners after him, but he was my first, and it was impossible for me to ever forget what it had been like.

I had woken up a few hours after we'd gone to bed. And I had woken up feeling the happiest and safest I could ever remember feeling...but it was something that I could never have again.

I had told him, there, in the quiet darkness of an early morning, that I loved him. Three words given to someone who wasn't even awake, a confession that I'd never have the courage to do if he'd been awake.

I felt the empty black hole inside of me. Even though it was just one night, I knew that I loved him wholly, deeply, and passionately — but it wasn't enough. I wasn't enough, and the knowledge felt like it would destroy me from inside, devastating me forever.

I cried silently as I whispered more that night. I told him about a fantasy life, one where he wasn't already halfway out the door. In it, we went to the same college, or at least one in the same town. My mother was happy that we were together, and Kyle and I got married right after we graduated from undergrad. We would have a kid maybe two years after we got married, and another one a few years after that. White picket fence. Golden retriever.

It was a nice dream, and it was one that had popped into my head after a single time with him. But it would never happen; it was a path never taken.

The one night that we'd spent together was written in indelible ink on a secret book that I'd tried not to open too often. It hurt still to think of him; he was the person I thought of at midnight when I was alone in my cold bed. And if I wanted to be completely honest, I'd say that I thought of him even on the nights when I didn't go to sleep alone.

I could hear Kyle's voice, part of the dream.

"I love you, Catherine. Please don't leave me."

I wanted to tell him that I loved him, too, but I didn't seem to have control of my mouth. I tried to open my eyes, but it felt like I had fifty-pound weights on them.

I gave up after a while, and I let the blackness take me back into oblivion.

Waking Up

Catherine

When I woke up again, I wasn't as foggy. I could open my eyes, and the first thing I saw was a ceiling that was not the ceiling of my bedroom in the condo. I remembered then that I was staying at Kyle's parents' home, but it wasn't that ceiling, either.

I could smell the scent of a hospital, and I knew where I was.

"You're awake."

I turned my head toward the voice. Kyle was sitting on a chair with a laptop in his lap. He closed the laptop and stood by my bedside. He put his hand in mine, and I knew in that moment that everything would be fine. He was my dream come true.

I tried to sit up, but I felt too weak.

"Don't move. You might pull your IV out."

IV? I looked around, and I saw that I was attached to a saline drip. "Why am I in the hospital?"

"You can't remember?" Kyle looked at me carefully. "You were in an accident."

I blinked. "A car accident?"

"Yes." Kyle's thumb stroked my hand lightly. "Someone ran into you when they gunned it at a green light."

I closed my eyes. "I can't remember any of it."

"Don't worry about it."

A nurse walked into the room, and she snorted.

"Get away from her. She's healing," the nurse scolded.

Kyle dropped my hand as if it were a hot coal. "Right. She's healing. Sorry."

I reached my hand out to him. "No, I'm fine."

"You're lucky that all you had were some cracked ribs. You really should've gotten more from a car accident...we didn't know the extent of your injuries at first, and we thought that one of your ribs might be puncturing your lungs." she clucked at me, but I stopped listening. Kyle was here now, and that was the most important thing now. That was the most important thing ever.

"When can she be discharged?"

Kyle interrupted the nurse, and she gave him a glare that should've made him burst into flames. "When the doctor says, and not a minute sooner."

I heard footsteps, and then a lady doctor wearing a white coat and a nice smile walked into my room.

"How are you doing, sweetie?"

"I'm okay. I just woke up. My ribs hurt."

The doctor nodded. "That's to be expected. Now that you're awake, let me do a quick check for a concussion." She fished a flashlight out of her pocket, and before anybody did anything, she shined a light into each eye and watched my eyes intently.

"Hey! Too close," Kyle barked, but the doctor just shook her head.

"I have to check her for a concussion, but she looks fine. Wake her up every four hours, and if something looks wrong, bring her back."

"So she can leave? Is that what you are saying?"

"Yes, she should be fine. I can start the discharge order set, and you'll be on your way within an hour."

The nurse looked like she had sucked on a lemon, but the doctor's authority definitely exceeded hers.

There was a lot of hustle, bustle, and paperwork before I could get out, but I finally did. They insisted on wheeling me out of the hospital, even though I could walk.

I got into Kyle's SUV, and he drove a little under the speed limit as we went home. When I realized that he was ten miles under the speed limit, I said, "I'm not made of glass, you know. It's fine to drive normally."

Kyle turned to me. "I won't take any chances with you." He touched my hand softly before putting his hand back on the wheel. "We're almost home anyway."

He hadn't taken me back to his parents' house, where all of my stuff was. Instead, we were at his home. I didn't protest. To be honest, even though I knew that Kyle's mom would fuss over me and take excellent care of me, I wanted to be with Kyle.

Regaining Strength

Catherine

I'd mostly stayed in bed for a while. I'd called into work, and I'd taken an indefinite leave of absence from the hotel. It wasn't ideal, since I hadn't been working long, but they gave me a free pass since I'd been in a car accident that put me in the hospital. They promised to have a spot somewhere for me when I went back.

Kyle had acted as if I were made out of glass. We had a housekeeper who did the cooking and cleaning. He kept me in the guest bedroom downstairs, and it made me lonely at night when I heard him walking around in his room, pacing, restless. I wanted to be up there with him, but I was too shy. Besides, what could I do with cracked ribs?

Kyle moved all my stuff from his parents' house to his own. I didn't protest, and I still got a nice call from his mother almost every day. She baked me apple pie and told me to get better. The day that I could breathe without hurting, I made a plan.

* * *

I walked upstairs after listening to Kyle pace around for a half hour. I couldn't take it anymore.

I opened his door, and he spun around.

"What are you doing up here? You shouldn't be going on the stairs."

I jumped onto his bed. "I'm all healed! See?" I bounced again.

"I don't want you to hurt yourself," Kyle said, frowning. "Stop it."

"I'm fine," I told him. "I'm not going to shatter into a million pieces. I'm not going to drive a car in the next few days, but I want you to know that I'm just fine."

I slid off of the bed, and I threw my arms around his neck. I kissed him, and he kissed me back while his hands went automatically to the center of my back, near the end of my rib cage, before he let go.

"No...this isn't safe for you." He gently pushed me about an inch away.

I stuck out my lower lip. I knew I was pouting, but I didn't care. "I want to kiss you. I need to be held. You haven't touched me since I had my accident."

"Your ribs were cracked. I didn't think that it was a good idea. Having you in a bed in my house is like offering rare steak to a hungry wolf...it's not going to be pretty and gentle, Catherine."

"I don't care. Eat me up."

He shook his head, and I noticed that his hands were slightly trembling. "No. I shouldn't."

I pulled him to the bed, and I twisted us around and then pushed his shoulders down so that his back was flat.

I kissed him again, and this time it was harder to resist. He stayed still for the first few seconds, but he started to kiss me back again.

I broke the kiss, then I got naked. He bit my neck, and then he bit my breasts.

"Do you want me? Do you want this?"

"Always. I'll show you."

His mouth traveled down my front, past my breasts, past my belly button, until he reached for my core. He pushed one finger inside to test how wet I was. I hadn't had sex in a while, and I was ready after we had made out.

Our eyes were locked as he sucked on the finger that he pushed inside of me.

"Delicious."

His head went between my thighs, and I had a small moment of panic. It felt so intimate.

But I couldn't think about it after a little while, because his tongue was doing things to me that made me feel like my entire body was on fire.

I melted beneath him, and he kept going as I crested again and again.

My body felt like it was made out of jelly by the time that he stopped.

He crawled so that he was behind me, and he was the big spoon. I could feel his hard erection digging into me.

"What about you?" I tried to turn so that I could grab him, but his huge hand on my hip stopped me from rolling over.

"Don't worry about me. Tonight was all about you."

I wiggled, and he kept me in place, but I could feel him growing.

"Stop moving." I could hear his breath coming in pants.

"I'm okay!" I said, and I rolled to face him too quickly for him to stop me. I put my top leg around his hips, and he involuntarily pushed his hardness where I needed it the most.

"I don't want you to get hurt."

"I won't...if it hurts, I'll tell you. I promise." I kissed him slowly.

There was a beat of silence. "Okay," he whispered.

I unbuttoned his jeans and unzipped him. I pulled out his beautiful rod, and I saw the drop of precome on the tip. I used it to pull on it a little.

"Stop that, or we'll be done before we get to the main course."

I settled back where I had started, with one leg over his hip. I guided him into my wet slit, and we both gasped as we felt our bodies fit together.

Now that he was inside of me, he couldn't hold himself back. His hand went to grip my hip hard as he crashed into me over and over again. It had been a while since we'd had sex, and it showed. His eyes were shut, and his mouth was open. I knew he was close, so I pulsed my muscles. I blessed the book that had taught me Kegel exercises.

With a shout, he spilled himself inside of me. I was surprised to orgasm when I felt his heat surge inside of my body, but we both lay there on the bed, waiting to catch our breaths again.

He eased out of me, and then he picked me up and brought me to the shower.

We didn't have shower sex. We just slowly lathered each other up, kissed a lot, rinsed off, and then snuggled in bed, pretending that the sheets were good substitutes for real towels.

Lana Thrice

Kyle

I locked the door behind me when I left. I left a note on my nightstand so that she would see it when she woke up. It only said, "I love you." It was simple, but I knew that it would put a smile on my girl's face.

I went into the office, and I tried to get my head into the game. I was a little behind from all of the drama with Catherine's accident, but it was enough to keep me busy.

I felt a tingle at the back of my neck, and I had the strange feeling of deja vu.

I looked up, and there was Lana, yet again. She was dressed to kill again, and I frowned. We'd been through this already.

I went out and, with a firm hand on her arm, guided Lana into my office.

"What are you doing here?" I frowned. "Dressed like this?"

"I want to get a drink with you."

"No. You stayed overnight in my house. What are you doing in town? I already talked to you about this. I don't want to date you or anything. I've got a serious girlfriend."

She walked swiftly out the door without saying a word. I didn't know if she was going to cause a scene, so I walked behind her. She went to her car. She had a Caillou sunshade in the window of her backseat.

Why did she have a Caillou sunshade?

She leaned into the backseat, and I could hear her murmuring quietly. She straightened up, and my jaw dropped to the ground.

She was holding a baby in her arms.

"Meet your son," she said softly.

I couldn't believe it. I hadn't slept with Lana in a long time, and I had broken up with her a very long time ago.

"Are you for real? That's my son?"

"Johnny, wave hello to your daddy."

I swallowed. Johnny looked a lot like Lana, and he reminded me of someone...but he didn't really look like me. He was ninety percent Lana, and ten percent something else.

Johnny buried his face in his mother's shoulder.

I came close. "Hey, little man." I stroked his back. "Don't be afraid. I don't bite."

I pulled him away from his mother, and he squirmed to get back to her and cried a little. I tossed him in the air gently a few times, and then he was ready to be held and cuddled by me.

I had to admit, this kid was pretty adorable. He had dimples and dark hair. I could see why this kid could be mine, but I hadn't really slept with Lana.

I flushed, remembering the last time that we'd been in bed. It had been a wild experiment — and one that I never repeated after that day — but there was a small chance.

"What do you want from me?"

"I want my child to have a father."

"Why didn't you tell me before now? How old is Johnny?"

"He's twenty months old. My mom helped me with Johnny when I stayed overnight at your house, but she doesn't have the resources to do it that often. I can't move in with her. She lives in a tiny apartment, Section 8 housing, and it would violate the terms of her agreement if I brought Johnny to live with her. And I lost my job last month...I'm running out of my savings."

I nodded. "We'll find a way to take care of this. Don't worry."

Lasagna

Catherine

The kitchen was hot, so I turned on a portable fan.

I stirred the lasagna mixture on the stove. I'd put it together and pop it in the stove when Kyle came home. Then we'd be ready for our meal.

The front door opened, and I went to greet him in my sauce-stained blue apron.

"Hey, Kyle. How was work?"

I frowned at him when I saw how pale he was. "What's wrong? Did something happen?"

"Nothing. It's nothing. What's cooking? It smells good."

"Just lasagna. Something went wrong at work today?"

"No, nothing went wrong at work. I need a beer."

He headed towards our fridge, and he popped open a Guinness and drank it down like it was water.

"Something happened, mister, and I want to know what it is...or you're getting none of this delicious lasagna." I quickly poured the lasagna mixture into the pan that I had prepared, and I layered it with the noodles. I popped the whole thing into the oven.

He put the beer down. "Lana came by the office today."

"What? Why? What did she want?"

"She..." He stopped, and he drank more beer. "She had something to say to me."

"What was it?"

"She said that she had my kid."

I gripped the granite countertop for support. "You made a baby with her? Didn't you date her in high school? How would that math even work?"

"No, the math doesn't work out. We dated in high school, and we haven't dated since..."

He stopped, and his face turned pure red.

"What is it? What's wrong?"

"Um...I don't know how to tell you this."

My instincts took notice. "What's going on?"

"Lana's pretty...open-minded. We may have had a..." He covered his eyes. "Threesome when she was dating my friend Kade."

"What?!" I could feel my breath coming in harsh gasps. It was like all the oxygen had been sucked out of the room. What was he saying? "What do you mean?"

"That's what she meant when she said that she didn't know who the dad was."

I sat down hard on the couch, and I covered my face with my hands. The baby that Lana was toting around could really be Kyle's. I knew when I'd gotten involved with him that he was a player, but this made it real.

"Okay." I cleared my throat. "What's your game plan? Our game plan?"

My words ignited a spark of hope in his eyes. "You'll stick with me through this?"

"Just until we know whether or not you're the father. I mean, there are only two candidates, right?"

Kyle nodded. "Yeah. It wasn't an incredible night...I didn't repeat it, ever."

"Stop talking. You're just digging yourself deeper."

Kyle mimed zipping his lips. "We won't talk about it again."

I shook my head. "Let's eat some lasagna. Change, and I'll put this into the oven."

I got the lasagna ready and put it into the oven. This wasn't the nice dinner that I'd planned. I had wine breathing on the counter, and I poured us each a glass. After I looked at the level of the wine, I added a lot more. We needed a lot of wine tonight. I took a sip of mine.

He walked back into the kitchen, and I don't know what possessed me to throw my wine all over him.

Hatred

Kyle

I grabbed her wrist. "What was that?"

She was crying. "I don't know…I'm overwhelmed…I feel like I don't fit into your life. You might have a baby. You had a threesome with your friend and his girlfriend, your ex. I feel like you're so much more experienced than I am, and I feel like I don't fit into your life."

"Of course you fit into my life."

"I think I should go."

"No, Catherine..." She tried to push past me, to go towards the door. But I pulled her in close, despite being wet with the red wine that she'd thrown onto me, and I kissed her.

She bit me.

I kissed her some more, and she melted slowly in my arms.

She was still crying.

"Catherine...I can't change the past. I'm sorry. But I'll be your future, if you'll let me."

"I just don't know." Catherine tilted her face up to mine, and I couldn't resist her sweet mouth. "I don't think..."

I kissed her hard. "Don't. Don't overthink this. Just let the two of us be right here. Forget about Lana and Johnny. Let's just be you and me."

"What are your plans, though? What are you going to do? How do I fit in?"

I kissed her again to make her quiet. "I don't have all the answers right now. This is new to me. But I promise you that you'll be part of my decision-making process. That's all I've got." I kissed her again, and I felt her arms wrap around me. She felt right in my arms, soft and sweet-smelling. I bit her ear, and I knew she liked it because she moaned.

All of a sudden, I couldn't wait to get inside of her and claim her as mine. She felt like she was pulling away, but she was mine. I'd been a fool not to claim her when I was getting ready to graduate, but now I was older and maybe a little bit wiser.

I reached under her skirt and tore her panties right off of her.

"Kyle! Do you have any idea how expensive..."

I shut her up with another kiss. I couldn't be stopped right now unless she outright told me no.

I flipped up her skirt as I lifted her onto my granite countertop.

"It's cold..." I knew she wouldn't feel it for long.

I spread apart her thighs as far as they could go. I rubbed her clit in slow circles while I attacked her mouth. Her hands were in my hair, and she pulled me as close as she could get.

I yanked off my pants, sending the button flying. I didn't care a bit. I was too focused on her.

I nudged my hardness into her center, and she moaned into my mouth as we kissed desperately.

Her thighs were clamped around me, and her hands slid down my back to grab my butt.

That was all it took for me to thrust into her, fast.

She screamed in front of me and arched her back. I bit her breasts as she panted. I loved the way that she was contracting around my rod.

Her hands pulled me close each time that I thrust, and I loved the smell of us together. It filled the kitchen along with the scent of lasagna.

I felt myself getting closer and closer, and I knew that I needed to speed her up. I captured her mouth and flicked my tongue inside of it. Then I rubbed her clit with one finger, and that's all it took. She writhed beneath me as her body was consumed by an orgasm. It was enough to pull me over the edge, and I grunted as I spilled into this beautiful girl, the love of my life, the one person I'd do anything to keep.

We were both catching our breaths when the timer for the lasagna went off.

I pulled out of her. I wet a paper towel and cleaned her up as best as I could. I wiped myself up, too. I'd do a more thorough job later. I pulled her off the counter. Looking at her, you could see from her smudged lip gloss and crazy hair that she'd been well loved.

"Stop looking so smug."

I put on an innocent expression. "Who, me?"

She slapped my butt. "I have to take the lasagna out of the oven."

I pulled up my pants, and I hoped that my belt would be enough to keep them in place.

She cut up the lasagna, and she put it on plates for the two of us. It smelled divine.

Before I took the first bite, I told her, "There's more." I used my fork to cut a small piece of lasagna and eat it. The spices really exploded in my mouth. Catherine was a great cook.

"What is it?"

I swallowed. "I still have to figure out custody."

She frowned. "Do you? I mean, the kid isn't really yours…"

"If it's biologically mine, then I'd like to be part of its life. And the baby is a boy. I want to be part of his life."

Catherine tapped her chin as she thought. "Then I'm coming with you."

"I'd like that." I grabbed her hand and squeezed it. "I'd love to have you along."

Park

Catherine

We got a text from Lana that night that Kyle should come to the park to decide what to do. So we showed up bright and early, and Lana was there with her little boy. He was running around on the playground while his mom sat on a bench in knee-high boots.

I had to admit that Johnny was adorable. He looked mostly like Lana, with cute dimples and an impish grin. He looked like a troublemaker, just like Kyle.

Johnny was climbing the ladder to get to the monkey bars, and he was too short to reach.

"Get down, Johnny, before you get hurt."

"Don't worry, Lana." Kyle went to hold Johnny around his middle. "Reach for each bar, kiddo. I've got you."

Lana and I watched as Kyle helped Johnny navigate the monkey bars that he was too young and too uncoordinated to actually handle. Kyle would be a fantastic dad one day.

I realized in a jolt that we'd been having unprotected sex. That seemed incredibly irresponsible. My only excuse was that I'd gotten very carried away.

When Johnny was done, he ran to the slide. Kids had so much energy. Kyle came back to Lana's bench, and he looked at me and indicated that I should take a seat next to him with a tilt of his head.

I went and sat next to him. I grabbed his hand to let Lana know that he was mine. From the side-eye she gave us, I knew that she had noticed.

"So what's the plan, Lana?" I asked her.

"Well..." She stopped. "Is it really necessary for you to be here?"

"She goes where I go," Kyle said firmly. "She's going to know everything that goes on. I can promise both of you that."

Lana looked unhappy but she nodded.

"What do you want from Kyle, Lana?"

"I want him to be a father to his son."

I nodded. "Okay, then. Is he on the birth certificate?"

"No," Lana answered, shaking her head. "He's not."

"So we should get a paternity test, then, right? So we can establish that Kyle's the father and get the birth certificate amended."

Lana looked really unhappy, and she played with a loose thread from her glove. "I don't think that's necessary. I wrote a will to make sure that someone would always be there to take care of Johnny in case the worst happened to me, and Kyle is listed as the father. Does it matter if he's biologically the father?"

Both Kyle and I blinked in sync. "Uh, yeah, it matters whether or not I'm the father. Hello! You told me that he was my son!"

Lana stood up. "Johnny! Johnny, we're going. Finish up. One minute."

Johnny nodded, and then he ran up the steps to go down the slide one more time.

"Lana, we need to get a paternity test so that we can put Kyle's name on the birth certificate."

"Okay," she whispered. "Just tell me when and where, and I'll bring Johnny there."

Johnny ran to his mother, and she picked him up. He was very tiny, and I could tell from the way that Lana held him close to her heart that Johnny was her entire world.

"We'll see you tomorrow."

She walked to her car slowly with Johnny looking over her shoulder at us and sucking his thumb.

I unlocked my smartphone, looked for a clinic, and showed the list to Kyle. "Where do you want to do the paternity test?"

He shrugged and said, "Wherever you want."

"Let's just go for the closest one."

"Okay. That sounds totally fine to me."

I got the address, and I used Kyle's phone to text it to Lana. I didn't know why he had her white bikini picture saved in his Contacts app, and it was better not to ask questions.

"Done. We'll see them tomorrow."

Clinic

Kyle

Catherine had kept me up all
night, which wasn't as appealing
as it sounded. She had tossed and
turned, crying a little whenever she
settled into place. I stared at the
ceiling all night, wishing that she
was sleeping downstairs again and
then mentally slapping myself for
thinking such a thing.

When it was time to get up, I
was tired, bone-tired, dog-tired.
But we needed to get to the clinic.

When we got there, Lana and
Johnny were already waiting.
Johnny had a G.I. Joe in one hand,
and Lana's eyes were red. It looked
like she had cried last night, too.

"Hey there, Johnny."

"Hi..." he said, sticking his
thumb in his mouth. He took it out
to ask, "Are you my daddy?"

"That's what we're here to find
out, buckaroo." I ruffled his hair.
"You can just call me Uncle Kyle
for right now."

Johnny extended his arms to me, and I picked him up and kissed him on his cheek. I could see that a bond was forming between the two of us, and it was definitely going to be interesting, no matter which way the test results went. He reminded me of someone, something about the stubborn chin that Johnny had, but I couldn't pinpoint it.

All four of us went inside of the clinic, and Catherine and Lana went to check in. I took Johnny to a table in the corner with a bunch of Legos. We made a bunch of Lego structures until a nurse came to call us into an exam room.

"What, no doctor?" I joked.

She gave me a glare that immediately made me regret joking at all. "You don't need a doctor for this."

"So how does this work? Do you do a blood test?" I started rolling up my sleeve, but she shook her head.

"Nope, I just need buccal swabs."

Johnny got pale. "What's a buccal?" He stuck his thumb in his mouth.

"Buccal means cheek. I'm going to swab your cheek with a Q-tip, okay?" Her tone was a lot gentler with a little kid.

"You can go first, okay, little man?"

Johnny ran to Lana, and she picked him up. "Mommy can hold your hand the whole time."

Lana set him on the examination table, and the nurse said, "Say ah."

Johnny opened his mouth, and the nurse carefully swabbed the inside of his cheek before putting the Q-tip into a Ziploc that had a label on it.

"Your turn, sir."

Lana took Johnny off of the examination table, and I hopped up. I opened my mouth wide. The nurse stuck a really long Q-tip in there, and she scraped pretty hard. I really shouldn't have tried to joke around.

"All done." She put the sample into a bag. "We'll send you the results as soon as the lab sends them to us."

"How long will that take?"

"Well, because this is a paternity test, it normally takes about a week. But you can expedite the results if you pay about twenty dollars extra."

"We'll pay the twenty dollars extra," Catherine blurted.

Lana and I looked at each other. Was it really that urgent?

"That's fine. Just tell the desk. I can mark these samples for expedited processing. You can get results in a day or two. I know that paternity tests can be pretty time-sensitive." She opened a drawer and gave a stick of sugar-free gum to Johnny.

"Thanks for being brave, Johnny."

"Hey, what about me?" I cracked. "I was pretty brave, too."

Her glare made me feel about two inches tall. "No."

Catherine drew me out of the room so that we could pay at the desk. "Stop it," she hissed. "She doesn't like jokes."

I was quiet when I whipped out my credit card. Man. The nurse at this clinic really didn't mess around at all.

"You'll get your results on YourChart as soon as we upload them. We'll call you when the results are ready, and you can log in." She printed out a sheet with a username and activation code. "We're trying to get all of our patients to receive electronic records."

Like a bank, I thought, but I didn't say it.

"Thank you," Catherine said sweetly. "We appreciate it."

"You have a nice day, now." She waved at us as we went out the door. Lana and Johnny were waiting by it, and the four of us went outside of the room together.

"Okay," I told Lana, "we'll call you when we get notified."

She nodded, and she carried Johnny to her car. I really wished that she had something bigger. He was so little, and I felt like he needed as much protection as he could get. I wasn't sure what it was about him, but he roused some protective instincts about which I hadn't even known.

"That's all over," Catherine said. She kissed my cheek. "Let's go home now and wait."

Test Results

Catherine

Two days after we did the paternity test, we got a phone call from the doctor's office. I put it on speaker so that Kyle could hear.

"We're here to notify you that you have received your test results in your account. Log into YourChart in order to see them. Do you have any other questions? You still have the activation code, right?"

"Yeah, absolutely." I'd put it somewhere... "I activated Kyle's account with him yesterday, so we should be set. Thank you for calling."

"No problem. I'll be contacting the mother of the little boy soon. Come back soon." The receptionist hung up the phone.

I hoped that we wouldn't need to. I clicked to access YourChart, plugging in the activation code from the sheet of paper that I'd put into my purse.

Phew. The results showed that Kyle wasn't Johnny's dad. I hoped that this entire thing was behind us, and Kyle and I could just move forward with our lives.

But that hope was in vain.

Less than an hour later, Lana was on our doorstep. She knocked, and I opened the door. Johnny was sleeping in a baby carrier. He was a precious tiny angel asleep.

"Can I come in?" She looked like she'd been crying, and she wiped her nose with her sleeve.

"Yeah, come on in." I hoped that this would be the last time that Lana came over.

"Just put the little one into the guest bedroom. I can pour you some juice or maybe something a little stronger?"

"Stronger is good." I watched as she went into the downstairs bedroom, and then I went to the cabinets, got some wine glasses, and pulled out a bottle of red wine from Kyle's stash. He had a fancy cabinet that tilted the bottles.

She came back, and she wiped a tear from the corner of her eye. She spotted the wine.

"Thanks for letting me in. I wouldn't blame you if you'd kept me out...after what I did to you."

"Just sit and drink. Let's figure out what your next steps are."

She lifted the wineglass, and she stopped. "Wait, did you put anything in this?"

"Nah." I grabbed that glass and gave her my own. "See? Not poisoned."

"I hope this isn't Princess Bride stuff. Oh well." She drank the entire glass quickly. "More, please. Thank goodness that I already weaned Johnny when he turned one."

I took the bottle and filled her glass up.

"So what's going on?"

"Well..." Lana looked around. "Where's Kyle?"

"He's at the gym right now. What's your plan?"

"I don't know. I really don't know. I thought that Kyle was the father. And now I'm just..." She wiped away another tear. "I have no idea what I'm going to do. I'm out of money, and I have a baby. It's a mess."

The front door opened. "Hey, Catherine. I'm home."

Kyle was sweaty, and I didn't have the time to appreciate it. "Lana's here."

"Yeah, I saw her car. What's up, Lana? Did we get the results back?"

"We did. Do you want to take a shower?"

"No, this is more important."

"Well, you're not the father." I gave Lana a little side-eye. "So Johnny isn't your child."

He ran two hands through his sweaty hair. "Okay. So what happens now?"

Lana was silently crying.

"That's what we were talking about when you came in."

"Lana, do you know what you're going to do?"

She shook her head, still crying. "No clue." She hugged herself. "I don't have anywhere else to go...nobody in my family has the resources to help with all of this. I just want to give Johnny the best I can, but I don't think that my best is that much. The baby is Kade's, and I just...I wish that he wasn't dead. I was in love with him. I know that if Kade was alive, then he'd take care of us. But I'm so lost."

Kyle looked like he didn't want to be in the room. "Um, I'm going to take a shower. Lana, why don't you come by for dinner around seven? We can make spaghetti...I'll play with Johnny...it'll be good. I need some time to process all of this."

Lana nodded, and she wiped her face. "That's fine. I'll get Johnny."

When she went into the guest bedroom, Kyle went to me and kissed my cheek. "Thanks for being a trooper," he whispered. "I really am going to take a shower. I'll find a way to make this right."

"Bye, Lana," he called.

"Goodbye."

She was still crying, and she had her sleeping son back in his carrier. My heart went out to her. It wasn't easy to be a single mother, and in that moment, I forgave her for lying to me. She'd do anything for her son, and who could blame her for that?

"Bye, Lana. We'll have a nice dinner, okay?"

"I'll see you later." She waved, and she walked out to her car.

I closed the door behind her, breathing a sigh of relief.

Kyle was already going upstairs for a shower. I needed more wine.

Shower

Kyle

I went into my shower, and I turned on the spray. I always did my best thinking in the shower, which had been a problem in the military, when water was pretty scarce.

What should I do? Johnny wasn't mine, which absolved me of responsibility. But for some reason, I felt like I still needed to take care of him. Kade had been a good buddy of mine, and I felt like I had a hand in Johnny's creation, even if I wasn't his biological father.

The warm water fell all around me, and I thought it over.

I knew that I wanted to help Johnny, and I knew that I would do so in memory of Kade...and because Johnny easily could have been mine.

What did kids even need? Warmth, shelter, clothes, school...I'd help with all of that. My parents were kind enough to give me more than I needed, and I didn't lead a crazy expensive lifestyle. So it shouldn't be too much to help out with Johnny.

What was Catherine thinking downstairs? She'd welcomed Lana in, and they'd talked at the table with full wine glasses like friends. I didn't know how Catherine felt about this whole thing, and I felt sorry for plunging her into this mess, my baby drama. But she was being strong about it, and it only made me love her more.

I got out of the shower and toweled off. My hair was a little longer than my regulation cut, but it still would dry pretty quickly. I put on a shirt and pants, and I went downstairs.

Catherine was drinking wine and poking her phone.

"Hey," she said, standing up. "What's going to happen now?"

"I'm not totally sure," I admitted, leaning in to smell her hair. She smelled so sweet all the time. "But I know that I want to take care of Johnny."

"What does that mean for me? Are you going to get back together with Lana?" She took a step back from me.

"No!" I almost shouted. I tried to calm down. "No. Lana's my past. You are my present and my future, but we're going to make sure that the little kid is taken care of."

She nodded slowly. "I guess I can see that. Johnny's a good kid."

"Yeah, he really is. And I was so close with Kade...I feel like it's only right for me to take care of his son, if he can't. He's never even met Johnny."

Catherine hugged me tight. "I love you. Just do whatever you think is best."

I lifted her off the ground and kissed her mouth. "I'll try to deserve your love and trust every day for the rest of my life."

I set her back on her feet. "I should get dinner started."

Catherine disappeared into our room while I put together spaghetti. It wasn't a strenuous meal, but it had a lot of stuff in it. I sliced and sautéed some mushrooms in a pan with onions and garlic, and the whole kitchen smelled pretty good. I cut up some Italian sausage and quickly pan-fried it. Then I put in some chunks of hamburger and browned the meat in the pan. I put everything together in the biggest pot that I had together with some store-bought meatballs, and I stirred in the tomato sauce that I kept in the fridge. It was my mom's, and there wasn't anybody in the world who could do a better sauce than she could.

All of it sat in that pot, getting hot and filling the kitchen with a fantastic scent. I parboiled some noodles, and I set them aside. I'd do the last bit right before we ate. Spaghetti was simple like that.

Dinner with Lana

Catherine

Right after seven, the doorbell rang. I went out to the front. Johnny bounded into our house. I was astounded by how incredibly confident he was. He knew that he was loved, and he didn't care where he was. He would greet each new experience with an open heart.

"Hey." I looked at Lana. She looked a little better than she had earlier that day, and she gave me a quick smile.

"Hey!"

She came inside, and she sniffed.

"Wow, it smells really good in here."

"Kyle did everything. I just set the table. Would you like some wine?"

"No, it'd probably put me to sleep. But if you have apple juice, Johnny and I would love some."

I nodded. We had some in our fridge. "Sounds good."

I took out a bunch of glasses and poured everyone apple juice. I figured if Kyle had it in his house, he might like it.

Dinner was light and fun. Johnny was a perfect way to relieve tension, and Kyle and Johnny goofed around all through dinner. I smiled. I knew that someday, Kyle would be a good father. I touched my stomach. Someday, we'd figure something out.

When dinner was over, I took out an apple pie. I'd picked it up right before dinner from a tiny German bakery that made amazing pastries.

"Wow, that pie is huge!" Lana exclaimed.

Johnny's eyes got big. "Big."

It was probably the size of half of Johnny's body, and he was not a tiny kid.

"Let's all get a slice." I cut a child-size slice for Johnny, but the rest of us got adult portions.

Lana ate it; when she was done, she sat back with her hand over her stomach. "Wow, I'm totally stuffed. Thanks for the amazing dinner, guys."

"Our pleasure." I started clearing plates, and Kyle ruffled Johnny's hair.

Johnny yawned.

"Okay, kiddo, let's go take a nap."

"Not sleepy," he protested, and he yawned again.

"How about this? I'll tuck you into bed and read you a story. You don't have to go to sleep, okay?"

Kyle picked him up, and he took Johnny into the spare room.

"Kyle and Johnny are a really good team," I commented to Lana.

She nodded. "They certainly are. I'm so grateful that Kyle is bonding with him. Let me help you with the dishes."

I washed, and she rinsed and dried the dishes. We got into an easy rhythm in the kitchen. It was quiet, but it was a comfortable silence.

Kyle came back out, and I smiled at him.

"He's asleep now. I think he's fine."

I washed and dried my hands, and I hugged him. "Great."

He sat back down at the dinner table. "I've got a plan."

Lana dried off her hands, and she sat back down in her seat.

"What do you want to do? I'm open to what you want. I'd like for you to be part of Johnny's life. He needs some kind of father figure."

Kyle nodded. "So here's what I think we should do...I want to help provide support for Johnny's living expenses. Let's say fifty-fifty. I'll reimburse you for whatever. We can set up a joint bank account only for Johnny's expenses, and I'll just refill it at the end of every month. How does that sound?"

Lana's hands were covering her mouth. "That's way more than I hoped for." She stood up and hugged Kyle. "Thank you for your offer."

"Sit down," he said, smiling. Lana went back to her chair. "I'm not covering all of it, so you do need a new job. But I think that it'll work out. I can talk to Catherine's boss about you sharing a job, and I think that you can have a simple schedule that pays you enough to take care of your son and gives you enough free time to spend the afternoons with him."

Lana started crying again, but I knew that they were tears of joy.

"This is incredible, Kyle. This is way more than I hoped for." She stood up and hugged him again.

I wasn't sure how I felt about it. Kyle seemed to be offering to take fifty percent responsibility for a child who wasn't his. Did that make him a good man or a crazy one? A little bit of A, a little bit of B. I knew that Johnny had triggered Kyle's protective instincts, and I cared about the little one as well. I'd do my part to make sure that Johnny grew up in a loving, supportive environment.

"I should go," Lana said, wiping her eyes. "I've been here long enough, and it's obviously past Johnny's bedtime."

She went into the bedroom, picked up her son, and gave one-armed hugs to Kyle and me before leaving.

After the door closed behind both of them, I turned to Kyle and kissed him. "I'm glad that Johnny is going to be part of our lives."

He leaned down to kiss me back. "Me, too."

Upchucking

Catherine

THREE MONTHS LATER

I woke up with a little tickle in my throat. It wasn't a cough. I ran for the bathroom before I threw up last night's dinner.

"Babe, are you okay?" Kyle came in and held my hair like I was twenty -one and unable to hold my liquor. I felt weak, and I lay on the ground. I didn't care how filthy it was. The cold tile felt good for me right now.

"I'm fine, I think. I think that I'm done barfing."

"I can stay home from work if you're sick."

"No, no. Don't stay home. You'll go to work. I'll go to work. And when you come home, I'll be better. It's just a little bug, that's all."

"If you have a little bug, don't stay here. I don't think that you should go to work if you're sick."

"I had to miss so much because I got in that car accident. I don't want to miss too much. They might as well fire me. It's a small mercy that I even have a job after leaving Aiden."

"They could, but they won't. Just stay home today. It's not like you want to get anybody else sick."

I sighed. He was right. "Okay. I'll stay home."

He patted me gently on the back. "I'm going to get out some ginger ale, okay? Do you need anything else?"

I shook my head. I closed my eyes and listened to Kyle going downstairs to get ginger ale for me. He was sweet, though I didn't need him to take care of me.

He was back upstairs in a minute with a can of Canada Dry. I stood up, went to the sink, rinsed out my mouth, then opened the can. The first sip tasted weird, but the second one tasted good. It was what my mother always gave me when I was sick.

"Thanks, Kyle." I put down the can of ginger ale. I went to hug him, then I remembered that I was sick. "Oh, I shouldn't hug you."

He hugged me around my middle and pulled me off the ground, touching my nose with his.

"I don't care if you're sick. I'm always going to be here to hug you."

I kissed his cheek. "Put me down. You'll be late to work."

He reluctantly let me slide down his body. "Go back to bed, okay? I want to see you feeling better tonight."

I nodded. "Don't worry. I definitely feel like going back to bed."

I crawled back into bed and closed my eyes. I heard him rattling around as he got dressed, then he kissed my forehead. I opened my eyes.

"I'll call your work and let them know that you are sick. Call me if you need me, okay?"

"Okay."

He walked out the door, and I closed my eyes again.

* * *

I woke up at twelve when my phone rang.

"Hey girl. Do you want to go out for lunch?"

I stared at the caller ID. "Lana?"

"Who else would it be?"

"Lana, I'm sorry, honey. I'm sick. I was throwing up this morning."

"Oh, no!" She sounded genuinely disturbed. She and I had really mended our fences over the last three months. Bonding over Johnny really helped. Kyle was a big part of Johnny's life, and the three of us made it work. Lana left Johnny at our house on Fridays, Saturdays, and Sundays, and we loved having partial custody of him. He was a delight to have around, and he was a very sweet and funny boy.

"You should stay away. I don't want to get you and Johnny sick."

"I am going to make you some chicken soup and bring it right on over."

"No, Lana! You'll get Johnny sick."

"How about this? I'll keep Johnny downstairs, and I won't even touch you. I'll just bring up a bowl of soup and then leave. I don't want you to be home all alone and sick."

The desire to keep Lana and Johnny healthy warred with the desire to be taken care of. I didn't have a mother anymore, and my selfish side won. "Okay."

"I'll be over in just a little while. Rest. I have my key." She hung up the phone, and I went back to sleep.

False Wall

Kyle

I went into work, and I looked around. As always, it was humming along steadily. Not for the first time, I wondered if anybody really needed me here.

When I got into my office, my dad was there.

"What are you doing here, Dad?" I looked around. "I didn't know that we had a meeting today. I would've shown up early." I unholstered my phone. No messages or missed calls. "What's up?"

"Let's talk about your future with my company."

I nodded. "Okay." I sat down behind my desk, and Dad looked at me for a minute.

"It seems like you fit in here. You've taken to it like a fish to water."

I shrugged. "Dad, it doesn't take a rocket scientist to push around a bunch of paperwork."

He smiled, folding his hands in his lap. "That's what nobody tells you about management. The higher up the chain you get, the less work you need to do. Often, the work that comes across your desk must be done urgently — and your decisions will impact a broad range of people — but the people who actually work for a crust are the ones on the ground."

"Are you sure about that, Dad? I mean, there are plenty of upper-level executives who seem to live in the office."

"Son, you just have to learn the art and science of delegation. You have a position that I personally carved out for you. We've got a hyper-loyal staff that's paid well for their trouble. They'll work for every minute that we pay them. That's the secret, son. If you can build a team that wants to see the business succeed, your business will succeed."

"So why are you here today? There really isn't much to do. I could probably be in here for a half day."

My dad shook his head. "It's about how it looks, son. Look at the people out there who are busting their butts for you. Do you think that they'd want to do that if they didn't see you here? No, you have to instill loyalty with a small amount of fear in their hearts. Fire first, ask questions later. It'll keep them to the standard that you require."

"But I have no idea what kind of standards that I should keep."

"It's unspoken at this point. These are businesses that I've set up, and these people are the kind that get cards and presents on their birthdays from me."

My dad touched a button in the wall, and it slid away.

"Wow, Dad. I thought that was an actual wall."

He wrinkled his nose. "Define actual." He waved his hand, and a computer whirred to life.

"Motion sensors, you see." He cleared his throat. "You've been doing simple office work. But here's the secret sauce: HR is the most important that you'll do with your time. I'm not talking about insurance or pensions. I'm talking about managing people."

Hearts and Minds

Kyle

I was totally stunned. He clicked a few times and put his thumb on a tiny fingerprint scanner.

"Dad, this is like CIA-level stuff." I blinked.

He clicked on a dossier. It was Jacob, one of the mechanics. It had details about him and his family — not just his wife and kids, but his other family members and everything that my dad knew about them.

"Did you get a private investigator to give you all this information?"

"Nope. What did you think that I did in the military?"

"You were...I don't know. I guess I've never asked. That seems weird, now that I think about it. You've never talked to me very much about your time in the military."

"I was in intelligence. A lot of the things I know I cannot tell you — they are still classified. But I can tell you that I learned a few tricks of the trade. A lot of us set up security firms when we got out."

"Is this even really a garage?"

Dad laughed, a belly laugh, a soul laugh. "It really is a garage, but there's a reason why you don't seem to be doing much work."

He closed the folder for this garage. "This is what my real job here was."

He swiped to another screen, and he scanned his thumbprint again.

"Dad, this looks like something from a television show."

I had no idea what I was looking at, but I had a sense that I shouldn't be looking at it.

"I got clearance to show all of this to my boy. You already had to go through security clearance to enter the military. You have a spotless record. It wasn't a hard push to get them to authorize you to have the same level of access that I enjoy."

"So, you have...a security firm?"

My dad grinned. "It's a lot more than that." He rubbed his nose. "I specialize in cars. Have you ever wondered why random Ferraris show up in a garage that mostly services Toyotas, Hondas, and Fords?"

"Because you're one of the only mechanics in the state who can take care of exotic cars?"

"Yes, that's true. But that's not the entire truth."

I was still totally stunned by what was happening. "Does Mom know about this?"

"She knows the shape of it, but not the specifics. She doesn't have time for this kind of thing. Did you not notice how busy your mother is in the local community? She does a lot more good than I do."

I covered my eyes. "This is so much to process."

"It's time that you got a real job, son." He smiled smugly.

I looked at my dad, and I realized that all of this had been his end game. He'd sent me off to the military to learn the hard lessons he'd learned. Then he brought me home to have the same kind of life that he'd led.

I stood up. "Dad, I don't think I'm going to accept this. I just think that a man should make his own way in the world."

The smile slid right off of his face. "If you don't do this, what'll you do instead? I don't have to tell you that finding people with the right clearance is a nightmare and a half."

"I don't know if I want to take a life on a silver platter. I don't know if I want to work for my old man...it feels like an easy pass. I'd rather make my own way."

"What will you do?"

"I'm not sure yet. Dad, clear that all away before anybody sees it."

Dad swiped his hand across, and the wall closed as the screen of the hidden computer went blank. "You're so ungrateful."

"You never asked me if I wanted what you could offer me. You put me through school...did you think that you were just educating me to be another you?" I shook my head. "I have bigger dreams than that."

His face was slowly turning red. "What's wrong with living my life? I happen to like it, thank you very much."

I checked for a last second that everything was tucked away, then I opened the office door. I headed home, nodding at everyone as I left. I told them that Catherine was sick, which was true.

Chicken Soup

Catherine

I heard the front door open.

"We're here," Lana called. "Stay upstairs. Johnny, please play quietly down here, okay?" I heard her drag out the playpen that we kept in our closet for Johnny's visits. He was happy enough in there. He had a huge box of toys. Kyle didn't understand the concept of "enough"; every time that Johnny came over, Kyle would give him a new toy. Johnny, if he really was Kyle's kid, would be the most spoiled child in the universe. I privately was glad that Lana had him, because showering Johnny with toys was fine for an uncle but not great for a father, unless you wanted to end up with Veruca Salt.

She stomped up the stairs. She had a Tupperware container of chicken soup and a spoon on a tray.

"Here you go. It's freshly made chicken noodle soup."

"That's so kind of you, Lana. I don't know how I got sick. It was all of a sudden...I felt fine yesterday, and now I feel so nauseous."

She sat down on the edge of the bed, and she smoothed the bedspread for a few seconds.

I ate a few spoonfuls of the soup while she thought.

"Penny for your thoughts."

She looked at me and flashed me a smile. "I know that this might be too personal, and just tell me if it is, but is there any possibility that you could be pregnant?"

The spoon dropped from my hand and landed on the tray. I steadied the tray on my lap.

"Pregnant?" I whispered. My mind whirled. We hadn't been using protection. It was an actual possibility.

With Aiden, I'd been careful about using protection. I knew that it would ruin whatever plans he had for me to have a kid too early. With him, I knew that his family would never forgive me for having the child too early. He was all about keeping up appearances — I was glad that I'd learned the truth about his parents' marriage before I'd followed through with ours.

"Maybe."

Lana smiled and patted my hand. "You can get a home pregnancy test from CVS, if you want to find out. If you have morning sickness, then you're far along enough to test positive."

I blinked a few times at her. I knew that she was speaking English, but I couldn't comprehend what she was saying.

"Pregnant?"

She moved to hug me, and then she stopped. "It's a real possibility."

I shook my head. "I'm going to need time to process that possibility. What's up with you?"

"Well, I met a guy..."

"A guy! What kind of guy?" I was glad that she was on the dating scene, and I was doubly glad because there was a small part of my heart that remembered what Lana had tried to do when she first came back to town. Now that we were friends, and she brought me soup, I valued her thoughtfulness, but I could never shake that moment that I'd seen her wrapped in a towel at Kyle's front door.

"His name is Ryan. I don't think that you remember him. I think he went to high school with us, but he came by my workplace...he's so tall. He's got these dark eyes that are so intense." She shivered. "I love it. I love being with him. He asked me out a week ago, and I've seen him every night since then."

Was there a Ryan in high school? I couldn't remember. It seemed too long ago...I'd met a lot of people since then, and it seemed almost like another life. My overwhelming memory from high school was my night with Kyle. "That sounds a little intense for someone you just met." I frowned. "Are you sure about him, Lana?"

She just laughed. "I can take care of myself. I'm pretty sure that he's harmless."

I was still frowning at her, so she got off of the bed. "Johnny is a little too quiet downstairs, so I'll let you rest a little. Believe me, I was really low on energy when I was pregnant with him." She waved goodbye, and I told her, "Be safe."

I put the tray on the floor next to my bed.

Ryan. Did I know a Ryan? That description seemed to trigger something in my memory, but I didn't know what it was. The question bounced around in my head as my eyes drifted shut.

Pregnancy Tests

Catherine

Despite Kyle's protests, I went into work the next day.

Nothing had piled up in my absence, so I just whipped out my phone and researched "How do I know if I'm pregnant?"

They talked about the symptoms of pregnancy, and they also talked about the partial reliability of home tests. I guessed that I should get one or two.

I spent all day thinking about what it would mean for me to have a baby. One, it would definitely change the relationship dynamics between Kyle and me. Two, it would change my entire life. Kids were a twenty-four-seven job, and the job lasted forever. I didn't know if I was old enough for that — I was still surprised to have an adult job. I passed the entire day in a haze, and I couldn't wait to get to a pharmacy.

When I was in the parking lot, I saw someone leaning on Lana's car. He must be Ryan, her boyfriend with the dark hair and dark eyes.

"Hello," I called. "Are you Ryan?"

"You remember me?"

I scrunched my nose. "Should I?"

"We went to prom together."

In a flash, I knew where I had heard of Ryan from high school before Lana mentioned him. He was handsome enough, I guess. He seemed to adore me in high school, which I had found deeply flattering at the time. I'd stayed away from Kyle, and Ryan had been a sweet and safe alternative. He didn't change girlfriends as often as he changed clothes.

He was a nice guy, so I nodded. "Oh, yeah, prom." I couldn't even remember what kind of dress I wore at the time.

"Hey!"

I spun around, and there was Lana coming out of the building.

"You two look friendly." She looked like she wanted to be in the circle.

"We went to prom together," I told her.

Lana's smile dimmed a few watts. "Oh."

"It was so long ago, honestly, Lana. I didn't even realize who he was at first."

I aimed a quick smile at Ryan. "It's incredible that he even remembers my name."

Ryan had no quick repartee. He just looked at me like a lion would look at a steak.

Ryan's intensity made the hairs at the back of my neck stand up. I rubbed the back of my neck, and then I told them both, "I've got to go. Take care, you two." I didn't sprint to my car, but I wanted to. I didn't look back, but I could feel the weight of Ryan's gaze on me as I went into my car.

I wiped all of that from my mind, and I got back to the mission at hand. I went to the pharmacy closest to Kyle's house. I bought two different tests, and I took them into the bathroom as soon as I got home.

They had different instructions. One said that I had to pee on the stick, while the other one had to be submerged. I didn't know if I had enough in me, but I used both of them.

Then I waited.

I washed my hands, and I went to the kitchen to get a glass of water. If I needed to retake the tests, I'd need to be well-hydrated.

I read a book while I waited.

I got so caught up that I missed the time that I was supposed to check. I hoped that the tests weren't time-sensitive.

I went into the bathroom, and there were the two blue lines on one and a positive result on the other. That was official. I was going to have a baby.

Well, I should probably check with a doctor. Or maybe buy more pregnancy tests.

I felt my heart rate start to pick up. I had no idea about anything to do with babies. I was an only child, and I didn't know if I could handle it. A child was a big responsibility, and there were so many ways to mess up.

I heard the front door open.

Heaving

Kyle

Catherine's face was as white as paper when I came home.

"Are you feeling okay?"

She forced a smile. "Just fine. Peachy keen."

"I'll make dinner, tonight, okay? You just rest. Do you need me to grab a garbage can for you?"

"That's very sweet, but I don't feel nauseous...just exhausted."

She patted my hand and gave me that smile again. She was way too tired, and maybe she was coming down with something serious. She'd been sick for a while at this point.

I pointed to my couch.

"Rest."

She walked to the couch, and she closed her eyes. I took my blanket, and I wrapped it around my love. I kissed one warm cheek, and she opened an eye.

"Just stay here. I'll take care of everything."

She kissed me lightly on the mouth. "Okay. I think that I can safely promise that."

I turned on the stove. I opened the fridge to see what we had, and I frowned. It was basically empty. I'd need to get more food, but I didn't want to leave Catherine at home when she was bone-tired like this. I still had some eggs, though, so it looked like we were getting breakfast for dinner. I planned to make scrambled eggs. My fridge didn't even have butter in it, so I hunted for the unopened bottle of extra-virgin olive oil that my mother gave me when I moved into the house.

I turned the stove on high heat to get the pan hot faster, and I put the oil on so that it would sizzle and tell me when the pan was hot enough to cook in.

"Kyle!"

I grabbed my kitchen trash can and ran to Catherine just in time for her to heave into it. She stopped throwing up a few seconds later.

"Could you help me get to the bathroom? I still have the taste of vomit in my mouth, and my throat is burning."

I scooped her up and took her to the bathroom. She rinsed out her mouth with a little water, and then she swished around some mouthwash.

"You've been throwing up for a little while. Maybe we should see a doctor."

She sighed. "I don't think I need to see a doctor right away."

"If you're sick, you're going to the doctor." That was final. I didn't like seeing her like this.

"Kyle, I don't think I'm sick at all."

"Then how do you explain throwing up?"

She covered her eyes with her hand. "I might be pregnant."

Pregnant

Kyle

That last word rocked me to my core.

Pregnant? I did a quick recall of the recent times that we had been together, and I realized that we hadn't been using protection. I definitely had boxes of condoms around — I bought them in packs of four-hundred — but I hadn't even bothered to use them with Catherine.

Suddenly, I was the one feeling woozy.

I sank to the floor and looked at Catherine.

"Pregnant."

"Are you okay?" She might've been the one who had just thrown up, but I felt like I'd just been bucked off of an angry bronco.

I grabbed the countertop and pulled myself to my feet so that I could give Catherine a bear hug. I didn't spin her around since she had just been ill, but I kissed her cheek.

"I am over the moon about it." I pulled her up and kissed her nose. "Listen, if you weren't sick, then we'd be doing a play-by-play of how it all happened." I kissed the space between her eyebrows. I couldn't believe it. "I feel like the luckiest man in the world. What do you need? Pregnant women have cravings, right? Do you want anything right now?"

"Just you." She kissed me on the cheek. "I just want you."

I carried her into the guest bedroom, and I laid her carefully on the bed. I closed the curtains. "Just rest now."

"I feel like I'm fine. I got it all out. I don't feel nauseous at all. You don't have to treat me like I'm made out of glass. I'll let you know."

She stood on the bed, which made her taller than me. She pulled me into a searing kiss that made me weak at the knees. No matter how many times we kissed, it still had the magic of the first time.

I broke the kiss. "You're supposed to rest."

"I'm fine." She took off her shirt, and suddenly all the air went out of the room. "I can show you."

Off went her bra, and her nipples were hard. I closed my eyes. I was a good man, and I wasn't going to do this.

"I should go."

Her mouth came down on mine, and she kissed me as I resisted. But who could resist Catherine? I was not that good of a man.

I broke the kiss, and I swept her into my arms, gently laying her on her back on the bed. Her big eyes looked up at me. I braced my hands on either side of her and kissed her neck. She arched up beneath me, and the sound that she made was the most beautiful one that I had ever heard in my entire life. I unbuttoned and unzipped her pants, and I got rid of them and her underwear.

She was naked now, all the way naked, bare dark skin in front of me like a feast. I kissed her softly.

"Are you sure about this?"

"Take me."

Instead, I pushed apart her thighs. I kissed my way down her body until I found what I wanted, her core. I gave a long, slow lick that touched all of her pussy.

"More."

She was a dirty girl. I rubbed her clit with one hand while the other helped me get my tongue deeper inside of her.

Her lower lips were clenching, and she thrust her hips at me. I rode her in a quick rhythm as she found ecstasy beneath me, never stopping as I loved her like this.

She gently pushed my head away when her hips stopped bucking.

"Too intense."

"We've only just started."

Love Afire

Kyle

I took off my shirt, pants, and underwear. I was hard, and going down on her had just made me desperate for relief.

She licked her lips, and I felt a tiny spurt of precome shoot out.

"I want it," she told me, her eyes afire. "Give it to me."

"Bend your knees."

She did as I asked. I braced my body on top of her, keeping her knees near my shoulders. I slid inside of her, which was pure heaven. It was like coming home from a long tour away.

I wasn't going to last long like this. I wanted her too much, and I was more than ready to blow. It was too soon, and I pulled out.

Her hips sought me, but I held her in place with one hand on her pussy, my fingers stimulating her clit. Her hips circled, and I rubbed her furiously.

"I want you inside of me," she wailed.

"I don't want to hurt you," I said. I had the urge to pound her, and that's why I'd kept her legs between us. But I was so close that I might shoot all over this bedspread.

"Get on the bed," she told me. A lady's wish was my command, and my pregnant woman was definitely even more important.

I lay on my back, and she straddled me. She had one hand parting her folds, and the other one gripped my cock and sliding it into her opening. I grunted, unable to hold back.

"I can't stop," I told her.

"Don't. I want all of you."

I stared into her eyes as she rode me, her full breasts moving as she rocked on top of me and blew my mind.

I shouted as the feeling overwhelmed me. I felt myself pulse as I spilled into her wet, warm body. She arched back, and she screamed. I was glad that I had my own house.

As she came down, still clenching around me with a few aftershocks, I rolled us so that she was beside me on the bed. I put one arm around her and held her close. I kissed her mouth softly.

"Thank you. That was amazing."

My fire alarm went off.

I could smell a little smoke. I ran down the stairs, and I went into the kitchen. I'd left olive oil on the stove while I made love to my girlfriend, my newly pregnant girlfriend. I turned on the fan in the kitchen. I winced, because the alarm still wasn't shutting up. It wasn't connected to the fire department — I hadn't bothered to get it set up when I moved in — and so I just got a chair and removed the batteries from my fire alarm. I opened the front door.

Slowly, the room cleared.

So much for dinner.

I sat on the couch and tried to breathe in the fresh air coming from the door.

What was I going to do? Catherine was pregnant now.

I wanted to make my own way. I had a little nest egg, but I didn't have the fabulous wealth that my parents had and I didn't want to rely on my trust fund. Without a job, Catherine and I would survive for a little while. I didn't want to keep her at subsistence level, though. I wanted Catherine and our baby to have the best of everything.

I made up my mind in that moment to go back to my dad. I knew that the work that he was doing was important, and I might as well be part of it. Was it a bad thing to take over the reins of a business that I could run? No, right?

I had to do whatever was best for the baby.

As the smoke cleared, my resolve firmed. I'd do whatever it took to take care of my little family.

Parking Lot

Catherine

Early the next morning, I waited until the song I was listening to on the radio finished before I got out of my car. As soon as I closed my door, I took a step back, with my back against my car.

Ryan was in the parking lot.

"Oh, hello," I said politely. "How are you doing, Ryan?"

He ran a hand through his hair. What was he doing here?

"I wanted to talk to you."

"Oh?"

"Yeah."

I waited for a few seconds before he spoke.

"I just...I was so into you during high school. And I thought that we'd go to the same college and work it out...get married, have kids, have a house, the whole nine yards."

I wrapped my arms around myself. The morning air sent a shiver down my spine. Or was it Ryan's eerie presence in the parking lot at this hour?

"Well, Ryan, that was so many years ago…honestly, I can barely remember what we fought about. I know that we broke up during prom."

He looked into my eyes, and my shoulders went back a half centimeter. There was something wrong in his eyes, something feral, something that made me a little scared.

"I still love you."

I was glad right then for the support of my car, because it wasn't the right thing to say. I had Kyle's little one growing inside of me, and it was absolutely inappropriate for Lana's boyfriend to say these things to me.

"I need to go to work." I started to try to get into the building.

His hand landed on my upper arm, pinning me against the car. "Stay. We have a lot to talk about."

I stomped on his foot, trying to remember what I'd learned in self-defense. He gasped from the pain, and I sprinted for the door.

When I got inside, I closed it fully. Ryan was scary.

The entire day was one catastrophe after another, and I barely had time to sit down. I felt nauseous, and I had a headache. But I kept going. I barely had time to eat my lunch before somebody put another disaster in my lap.

I was very relieved when the clock said that it was five.

It was dark outside. With a full-time job, I barely saw any daylight during the winter. There was a weird fog outside, obscuring anything that was more than a meter away. I hoped that I could find my car. I wasn't the best at remembering the location of things. I could barely find my way around with a GPS, and fog just made things harder. Who knew where I'd end up tonight?

I felt like a metal wall hit me in the face. It rang my bells and made me see stars. Before I could do anything, there was a gag in my mouth. I was in a headlock, and a man towed me backwards, the cold metal of a gun pressed against my temple.

"This is what you get for running away," he said quietly. I stilled, terrified to my core. It was Ryan.

"Catherine! Catherine?" I could hear Lana coming nearer to us, and I struggled harder against Ryan's grip. He didn't loosen up even a millimeter. I wanted to warn her to stay away, but I could hear her walking closer and closer.

Ryan was choking me in earnest now, and I was barely hanging onto consciousness.

"Catherine?" Lana was finally close enough to see me. "Is that you?"

She must have noticed the gun, because she screamed.

But she was too late. The echoes of a gunshot rang out in the parking lot.

Peanut Butter and Chocolate Cookies

Kyle

"Where's Mommy?" Johnny asked me, sticking his thumb in his mouth. I gently tugged his hand out of his mouth. Lana discouraged thumb-sucking, and he had a security blanket to make him feel safe. I grabbed it and wrapped him up.

"Mommy should be home now." Lana had left to pick Catherine up an hour ago. They should've been here already. I didn't know if I was being paranoid, but I had a feeling that something was wrong.

I'd texted Lana a half hour ago, but I didn't have a read receipt. Catherine hadn't been answering any texts all day, and I figured that she'd been busy. But it was way later than she should be home on a normal day.

Lana had come over to drop off Johnny for the night, and I'd asked her to pick up Catherine while I finished cooking dinner. We were having mushroom risotto... if Lana and Catherine ever came home. Catherine got nervous when visibility was reduced, and the fog was pretty thick. Having grown up here, Lana knew how to navigate the streets when fog obscured everything. Johnny had been asleep when she left, and he was only now coming out.

I turned off the stove, having learned my lesson about leaving it on. I was fortunate that a bunch of smoke had been the worst of the damage. I moved the food off of the hot burners.

"Do you want to visit my parents, Johnny? I'm sure that Mom will bake cookies with you if you ask nicely."

"Cookies?" Johnny's eyes lit up with pleasure. I envied his childish innocence at that moment, because not even freshly baked cookies could distract me from the growing gut feeling that something was very wrong.

"Cookies," I told him firmly. I texted my parents that I was coming over and leaving Johnny.

I unlocked the kitchen door with my key, and my parents were sitting at the table and drinking a little bit of Guinness.

"Hi honey. Why do you have a little one, and why are you leaving him here?"

That was right. They didn't know what was going on.

I set Johnny on the ground, and he clung to my leg, a little shy in this new environment.

"This is Johnny. He's Lana's son...do you remember her?"

"You dated in high school."

"That's right." I nodded, and I itched to find Catherine. "Johnny was going to have a little sleepover at my home, but Catherine and Lana have both been missing for a little while. I feel a little silly, but I want to check it out. Could you bake cookies with Johnny? I promised him that you would."

"Of course," my mother said, and I thanked the stars above that my mother was an angel. "Do whatever you need to do, sweetheart."

She knelt in front of Johnny, and she looked into his eyes.

"Hello. I'm Mrs. Richards. Do you like chocolate or peanut butter better?"

He held my leg a little tighter. "Both."

"Then we'll make cookies with both. Come on. You have to help me get the chocolate out." She stood and walked into the pantry.

Johnny's gaze went up to meet mine, silently seeking reassurance that my mom was safe.

"Go have fun baking cookies, Johnny."

Johnny scampered after my mom. The promise of chocolate and maybe even peanut butter was very appealing.

I slapped my dad on the back, and I walked out to my car. I headed for Catherine. The worry was gnawing at me now in earnest, and I knew that I wouldn't be able to fix it until I saw Catherine healthy and safe.

Too Late

Kyle

When I got to Catherine's workplace, a scene out of my worst nightmares was unfolding. Catherine was on the ground, and Lana was too.

I don't know how I had the presence of mind to call nine-one-one and give them my location. Maybe it was my combat training.

I didn't have a gun, and Ryan did. But no gun could ever stop me from avenging my pregnant girlfriend and friend.

I'd been taught that twenty-one feet was the distance that I could run before a shooter could get off a shot.

I used the fog to hide and get closer before Ryan realized that I was in the parking lot. I wondered why there wasn't anyone else out here after they heard the gunshot. Maybe they figured that it was a car backfiring.

I had a Swiss army knife. It wasn't much, and it was laughably small. It wasn't meant for the use that I was going to put it to now.

When I was close enough to Ryan, I tackled him, knocking the gun out of his hand. I hit it so that it skidded away. I couldn't see it then, but neither could he.

Ryan was a little bigger than me, a little taller, a little heavier. But I had the strength of desperation, a small knife, and the overwhelming urge to protect my family from this madman.

We rolled over and over again. I slammed him into the ground. He must have had some kind of training, because despite being dazed, he kept moving and dodged my knife.

I hit him with a hook that went under his chin and knocked him out. He went still. I checked his pulse, and I knew that he was done. I rolled over his dead weight by pushing at his hip and shoulder, just like I'd been trained. I hadn't been trained to take off my belt and tie his hands together, though.

I knew that the police would be on their way soon. I went to Catherine. She was out cold, and I pulled her into my arms. I pinched her cheek a little, and her eyes fluttered open.

"Kyle. You have to help Lana." She pointed in Lana's direction. "She's hurt. Shot."

It seemed that Catherine and the baby were fine. I eased her out of my arms. It took a single second to see that I couldn't help Lana. A huge puddle of blood was around her head, and I knew she was gone.

An ambulance came, the sirens cutting through the air. A police car was right behind, with the lights blinking everywhere.

"Hands up," said a gruff voice coming out of the fog.

"I'm Kyle Richards. I'm the one who made the call." I kept my voice calm. I was guessing that they didn't know who I was. "Ryan is tied up. Catherine is fine, but Lana has been shot in the head."

"Stay right there," the voice commanded. "Get on the ground, facedown. Put your hands behind you."

I got on the ground, and I lay facedown. I heard the click of handcuffs as the cold metal closed around my wrists. It was a small price to pay for someone to pick up Ryan.

It didn't take long for them to see Lana. They loaded her on a gurney, and I shook my head. She was beyond saving.

Catherine, Ryan, and I took a ride in the back of two police cruisers. I figured that Ryan was pretty harmless since he was unconscious, so I asked that Ryan share my cruiser.

It didn't take long at the police station for Catherine to confirm my story from the 911 call. Ryan had some kind of warrant out for his arrest, and he was going to stay overnight. Catherine and I were released, and we went straight to the hospital.

We asked where Lana was being held, and they told us that she was already in the morgue.

Catherine buried her face in my chest, crying.

"She's dead. Dead!"

"I know." I stroked her back. I couldn't give her anything more than that.

When she stopped sobbing, she said, "Johnny's an orphan."

"I know."

"What's going to happen to him?"

"In the immediate future? He's at my parents' house eating peanut butter and chocolate cookies. Beyond that, I'm not sure what will happen."

Shock

Catherine

I was shaking a little bit. "I want to adopt him."

"The adoption process is long and very involved. Are you sure about this? I think that Lana's mom could probably take him. It would be tight but doable."

I shook my head. "I think that Johnny should be with us."

"We'll talk about it. Let's get you home." He put his hand on my stomach, and he felt it gently. "Is the baby okay, do you think?"

"Ryan didn't hit me there. He just choked me a lot."

Kyle touched my throat, and I winced. "Be careful; it's still tender."

Kyle growled a little bit. "He never should have touched you. Seriously, do they have no security at all?"

"The visibility was bad...I doubt that the security cameras could see in the fog."

Kyle had no response, but he looked grumpy.

"Let's go home." I tugged him lightly towards the door. "I am exhausted."

Kyle called a taxi, and we went home. Kyle's mom could drive us back to our cars tomorrow, but for tonight, we'd stay in the house.

I cried as we drove home, leaving Lana's cold body behind. I couldn't believe that her life could be snuffed just like that from a random madman. She had trusted him too easily.

When we got home, Kyle unlocked the door.

"I need to take a shower," I announced. I needed to clean Ryan's grime off of me. I had random bits of gravel on my skin, and I knew that I would feel better after a hot shower.

"I'll join you."

I started to protest, but I saw the look in Kyle's eyes. He probably thought that I'd collapse from exhaustion and shock. Maybe he was right. All that had happened today hadn't really sunk in.

I went upstairs to the master bath and got undressed. Kyle got undressed, too.

I started crying again in the shower, and Kyle didn't make me stop. He just held me in the safe circle of his arms as the water pounded down all around us.

"Lana's dead," I told him.

"Yes, she is."

"Why?"

Kyle didn't have an answer for me.

When the hot water ran out, he turned off the tap. He got out first, and he turned around and handed me a towel. I dried off, and I wrapped the towel around me.

I brushed my teeth and used a little cleanser. I got dressed in one of Kyle's shirts, and I went into our bed. My teeth were chattering a little, and it wasn't from the cold.

Kyle slid under the sheets. His heavy arm settled around my ribcage.

"Sleep."

"I can't," I whispered. "I don't know if I'll ever sleep again." When I closed my eyes, I felt the cold gun against my temple and heard the gunshot that had taken Lana's life in a half second.

Kyle held me there for several hours as I cried into my pillow.

Getting Johnny

Kyle

Bright and early the next morning, I slid out of bed. Catherine opened her eyes. She'd slept less than I had.

"I've got to get Johnny. This is the first night that he's ever spent away from his mother, his elderly grandmother, or us."

Our eyes caught. We knew that there would be a lot more nights that Johnny wouldn't spend near his mother. He didn't even know yet — I hadn't talked to my parents — and I knew that it would be a hard conversation.

Catherine and I got dressed quietly, and we went to my parents' house.

The kitchen smelled like blueberries. Mom had fixed her specialty for Johnny, and there was syrup all over his little cheeks. He had eaten breakfast with more enthusiasm than accuracy.

"Good morning, Mom." I hugged her. "How did Johnny do last night?"

"We watched Thomas until his eyes shut." I nodded. Those Thomas the Train videos must be ancient, but they must have still worked. They used to knock me out.

"Uncle Kyle," Johnny squealed. I dropped a kiss on his little head.

"Hey kiddo." Johnny was alone now, and I felt a surge of protectiveness. No matter how it shook out, I'd take care of him the way that Lana and Kade would've wanted.

I'd find a way to handle the hard questions later. Right now, I needed to eat my mother's excellent blueberry pancakes.

All of us sat down in the little kitchen nook, and we ate as many blueberry pancakes as we could handle.

Epilogue

*But I heard him exclaim, 'ere he
drove out of sight,
"Happy Christmas to all, and to all
a goodnight!"*

I closed the book. "It's time to go to sleep now, kids."

"But Mommy!" Johnny wailed. "One more story!"

My little boys were both valiantly trying to stay awake, but I knew that they were about to go to sleep. They were blinking slowly, and the blinks kept getting longer and longer as they struggled to keep their eyes open.

Jeffrey covered a yawn with his little hand. "Yeah, one more story!" He opened his eyes wide, as if that would stop him from going to sleep, and then he said, "I'm thirsty."

"None of those tricks now, kids." I kissed both of them on their foreheads. "The sooner that you go to sleep, the sooner Christmas will come."

"In the morning, will there be presents?"

"Well, if you have been good this year, and Santa leaves your presents under the tree. But you have to be asleep, or he won't come. He is a secret, you see."

"I want to meet Santa!" Jeffrey said.

"You can't meet Santa. The nicest thing you can do is leave him a card and some cookies and milk. That's why we baked a lot of gingerbread cookies."

Jeffrey's eyes were closed. Johnny looked like he wanted to protest, but when I gave him a glare, he obediently closed his eyes.

"I'll see you both in the morning. We can open presents before breakfast."

I turned off the lights in their bedroom. We had a spare bedroom downstairs, but the boys weren't old enough to sleep on their own yet. We had tried, when Johnny had turned five, to put him into the spare bedroom. He had cried, because he was afraid of the dark, even with a nightlight. It was better to have both kids in one room.

I walked downstairs, and Kyle was washing the dishes. "Are the kids asleep?"

"They seem sleepy, but they really want to meet Santa."

"I guess that we need to be sneaky about it this year."

"I'm going to wait until they are really asleep." I heard the creaking of floorboards upstairs, and I went out to the mezzanine. I could see two little faces watching the fireplace expectantly, waiting for Santa to come down the chimney. I smiled. I just had to wait for them to fall asleep. Johnny snored when he slept deeply, so I knew that I would hear it when the kids finally fell asleep.

"Let me dry the dishes, and we can put them away. That Christmas Eve party was fantastic, but I don't know if I can handle it next year. It's a lot of work, and the grocery stores closed early today."

When the last dish was put away, Kyle put his arm around my waist and kissed me softly on the mouth.

"While we wait, why don't we find an easy way to pass the time?"

I waggled my eyebrows at him, and we laughed. Abruptly, I was very glad that the sound-proofed guest bedroom downstairs was empty. Kyle had been an aspiring one-man band, and we still kept all of his musical equipment in the closet.

When we got into the bedroom, Kyle felt around for a spare red ribbon from our Christmas-wrapping station. He offered it to me.

"Just what are you planning on doing with that, sir?"

He leaned in to whisper in my ear, and his bristles turned me on as they rubbed against the sensitive skin of my neck.

"I'm going to wrap you up." He kissed me, then he pulled my hair into a ponytail before tying a bow in my hair.

"You are the best Christmas present ever," he whispered.

I took off my sparkly party dress, and I yanked down his zipper. He carefully undid his belt, and I leaned down to take him into my mouth. I loved the way that he smelled.

With that, I bent towards him. I always loved the taste of him. Earlier in our relationship, we had kept track of who gave oral. He'd won by a mile, because he loved the taste of my lower lips and was a lot sneakier about getting me to lay back.

I loved the sounds that he made, sounds made even sexier by how hard he was trying to suppress them. I licked the sensitive head in a slow rhythm, and his hips bucked upwards. His cock hit the back of my throat, and I tried to loosen my muscles so that I didn't gag on him. His hands were tangled in my hair now, and I knew that he was getting close. After several years of a very active sex life, even after we adopted Johnny, I knew his triggers.

I put my hand down to caress his balls, and it was over. He spurted into my mouth again and again, and I sucked down his salty, delicious come.

"Your turn." I was suddenly on the bed, totally prone on my back. My thighs were pushed as far apart as they would go, and he attacked my core like a starving man, like we hadn't just eaten way too much only a few hours ago.

I bit my lip to try to contain myself, but I knew that a few moans were escaping. When I came, my mind exploded into a million pieces of light, and I panted on the bed, totally exhausted.

He turned me over, and he pulled two pillows from the top of the bed to slide under my stomach to support me. I was on my hands and knees. He loved this position, and so did I. He got even deeper like this, and I just loved it when he went wild. He loved the smooth curve of my hips, more womanly now that I'd had a baby. I might have had a few light stretch marks in the aftermath of having a kid, but he didn't seem to mind. He bit and licked the stretch marks on my hips, and he had told me once that there was nothing sexier than making love to the woman who had borne his child.

He went down on me again from behind, touching my clit with one hand and putting his tongue into my pussy with the other. I felt like a fire was raging inside of me, and he pushed me into a small orgasm. I couldn't support myself on my arms anymore, because they felt like jelly; I collapsed so that my cheek was on the mattress.

Before I was done orgasming, he slid inside of me. Even after so many years together and having a baby, he still felt gigantic. I knew that he stretched me to my limit, and I totally loved it. He was the best thing that ever happened to me.

His hand found my clit again, and he stimulated me into another orgasm. I didn't know how much more of this I could take, but I would happily die of an orgasm.

It looked like he wouldn't be able to last forever though. He plunged into me as deeply as he could, and he moaned quietly as he emptied himself inside of me. After Jeffrey had been born, I went back on birth control. I knew that I wanted a second child, but Kyle wasn't a big fan of that idea. Jeffrey had required a C-section, and Kyle had accidentally looked while they took my insides out in order to get to the baby. Every time that I talked about another kid, Kyle went white. He loved Jeffrey, but not enough to put me in danger again. I told him that I was fine with it, but he was insistent that he would never put me in that position again. So I was on birth control for the foreseeable future.

I basked in the glow of his love, warming me from the inside out. My whole body felt like it was made of sunshine on a clear day. He turned us so that his arm was around me, cupping one breast as his big, hard body spooned behind me. He still trained like it was his job. He bit my ear, and I shivered. His cock was still inside of me, and I felt him getting hard again.

"You're insatiable," I told him.

"Only with you. Only for you," he whispered.

This time, we made love slowly and sweetly. He got hard again, and he pulled his hand away from my breast to cup my clit and rub it a little. It also gave him the opportunity to completely control the pace, as he rolled his hips into me over and over again.

I closed my eyes and savored the sensation. It was better than hot chocolate on a snowy day.

He bit my shoulder hard to muffle his own shout as he slowly came. The warmth and feeling of his come shooting inside of me made me shiver as I fell over the edge again.

This time, I got up. I thanked my past self for storing our spare baby wipes in here, and I opened a box so that we could quietly clean up.

I touched him reverently as I wiped him up, and I was so glad that Kyle had chosen me all those years ago. He took a wipe and washed me as well.

We fixed our clothes, and we walked out of the guest bedroom. His arm was around my shoulders, and he pulled me close. We barely fit through the hallway, but he made it work.

As we walked through the kitchen, towards the great room, I could hear Johnny's snores. When we got into the great room, I could see that both of the boys were fast asleep on the ground.

I hustled back into the guest bedroom and pulled their presents out. We tried not to spoil the kids too much, so they had been involved in buying some Christmas presents listed on the paper angels on the Christmas tree in the lobby of our church. I reminded them that there were children who were less fortunate, and they seemed enthusiastic about giving toys, boots, and coats to kids who didn't have what they did. It was all part of the holiday spirit.

Jeffrey had a board game that he was obsessed with at school, and he cried when we took him home and pulled the game out of his hands. We bought it for him, and I hoped that there would be fewer scenes now when we picked him up from preschool. Johnny was a big fan of Cars, which we'd watched what felt like a million times, and we bought a huge set of Hot Wheels for him. I knew that I'd spend the next few months cleaning them up from every conceivable nook and cranny, but it was worth it to see Johnny's face light up on Christmas.

We still celebrated Lana's birthday as a family. It was important for Johnny to remember where he came from. But as time went on, his memories of his mother seemed to fade more and more. So, I took videos of him telling me all that he could remember, so that he could keep her alive that way.

I put their presents under the tree, and I noticed that Kyle was busy, too. He was quickly eating all of the gingerbread cookies that I had left for Santa.

I frowned at him and pinched his arm. I whispered, "Stop it, Kyle! Let me have some, too."

"Sorry, babe. I'm starving. You gave me a workout."

He gave me a wink and the last cookie, and then he drained the milk. I shook my head, but I quickly ate the last gingerbread cookie. I was glad that I'd put a little orange zest into them. It really changed the taste of the cookies and made them better. Orange peels were very bitter, but it definitely helped enhance the flavor of gingerbread.

Right then, I heard the clock chime midnight. Kyle kissed me slowly.

"Merry Christmas, love." He let go, and I slid down his body.

I got up on my tiptoes and kissed him a second time.

"The kids are going to be up way too early tomorrow, probably before dawn. Let's go to bed."

The two of us carefully went upstairs, careful on our creaky stairs. Kyle picked up Johnny, and I picked up Jeffrey, careful not to wake up the kids. We tucked them into bed. Kyle and I went to bed in our master bedroom at the end of the hallway. I should've showered, but it was all that I could do to brush my teeth and use some cleanser. I fought my eyelids, which seemed to weigh a ton.

I took off my clothes, put on my Christmas flannel pajamas, and crawled into bed. This was a pretty cold month, but I had Kyle to keep me warm. He lay behind me, and his big body was so much bigger than mine. His arm curled around my rib cage. He kissed my neck, and I felt little flames radiate from Kyle's lips.

"Good night, darling."

"Night."

I let sleep take over, ready for Christmas morning.

* * *

"WAKE UP! WAKE UP! IT'S CHRISTMAS!!"

I cracked open one eyelid. Johnny was jumping on the bottom of the bed. Jeffrey wasn't big enough to climb up, but he was certainly trying.

"What have I told you? If the sun's not up, Mommy isn't up."

"But Mommy, it's Christmas!"

"Have you brushed your teeth yet?" I asked, as sternly as I could, considering that I'd been awake for all of thirty seconds.

The two of them went running to their bathroom. Jeffrey still needed to use a step stool to reach the sink, and Johnny was proud that he was big enough to reach everything in the bathroom. It was crazy, because it wasn't that long ago that I gave him a nightly bath. He'd only started doing it for himself last month. sHe was growing up fast, and I wished that Lana could see him now. I silently thanked her for entrusting her son to Kyle and, by extension, me.

They must have broken the speed record for brushing their teeth, and I suspected that the two of them would have stinky breath later on, but they came back in about a minute.

"Presents!"

Johnny jumped on the bed and tackled Kyle.

"Ungh!" Kyle complained. "No. Stop. Five more minutes."

"BUT IT'S CHRISTMAS!"

"Inside voice, please, Johnny."
I considered telling him to stop
jumping on the bed, but if I had to
be awake at this hour, then Kyle
had to be there to share the
Christmas morning misery. Joy.
Whatever.

"Presents?" Jeffrey put his
thumb in his mouth.

I tugged his thumb out of his
mouth. "Let's go downstairs and
open presents. No running."

I watched my two boys walk
very quickly downstairs. Jeffrey
had to use the banister carefully,
but Johnny was downstairs before
I could catch up.

Kyle trailed me as we followed the kids downstairs, and Johnny picked up the box clearly labeled *Johnny.*

"Mine?"

"Yup." He'd only learned to spell his own name a little while ago.

He tore open the wrapping paper, and his eyes bugged out when he realized just how many cars he had.

"Wow!" He danced a jig in the way that only small children could. "Thanks, Santa!"

Jeffrey was a little slower to open his present, bewildered by the wrapping paper. I had to help him, and I carefully slid the box out of the wrapping paper.

"Game," he told me solemnly as he hugged the box.

"Yes, Santa brought you the game that you like so much."

"Like," he told me.

Kyle came beside me, and he slung an arm around my shoulders. Jeffrey climbed into my lap.

"Happy, Mommy."

I kissed his sweet-smelling little baby head.

"Happy Christmas, baby boy."

Johnny wasn't going to be left out. He climbed onto Kyle, Hot Wheels forgotten. "This is the best Christmas ever, Daddy Kyle!" He flung his arms around Kyle's neck with more enthusiasm than precision, and I had to dodge his little hand as he flailed around a little bit.

I smiled at our two sons. They were beautiful children, sweet and easy most of the time. I was so happy to be here with my three boys, joyous and safe on Christmas morning.

THE END

www.ingramcontent.com/pod-product-compliance
Lightning Source LLC
Chambersburg PA
CBHW052348020726
47503CB00001B/158